//Never in Her Arms\\

by

CHARLES NUETZEL

WRITING AS "JOHN DAVIDSON"

The Borgo Press
An Imprint of Wildside Press

MMVII

//<u>Contents</u>\\

//**Introduction**\\

I just happened to like this title, for it implies so much. Whether the story lives up to those implications, I don't know. But it was one of those books which kinda wrote itself.

What we have here is one of those contemporary tales about people trying to climb from nowhere to success. And it shows how there are different kinds of love, some of which are positive and others dangerous nightmares.

This is a study of how a woman can totally capture a man's hunger and feast on his soul to satisfy her own selfish needs.

Paula Martin becomes an obsessive object of desire to our hero, Peter Scott. To make things worse, she's his boss' sister-in-law, and has the power to make or break his career.

To me as a writer, that's interesting enough. I'll confess: I'd hate to have a lovely lady like this tossing herself into my arms and saying: *I'm yours, luv, no questions asked. Let's have some fun!*

One can't blame any man finding her attractive and desirable; and thus it is easy enough to understand my hero's attraction to her.

Never in Her Arms reveals how obsession can shatter relationships and create havoc in the lives of those it touches. It is, also, a story of romance and ambition, for it tells the story of an ambitious young man in love....

Peter, for the first time in his life, was facing great changes and challenges: a new job, and what seemed a wonderful future with Joanne Nestor, a sweet enough woman he'd known for years. She was a nice companion and caring lover, and they planned on someday getting married.

But, of course, nothing is that simple.

Paula had ideas of her own. When she met Peter it was instant desire. The overwhelming attraction ran both ways. After their first night together he knew what had been missing with Joanne: wild, unrestrained passion. Paula was like an addictive drug, and a dangerously unstable female. And once her claws had sunk deeply into his soul, he was lost in a whirlpool of crazed hunger that wouldn't let go.

Escape would come at a terrible price! And murder could follow!

When tragedy struck, Ann Fenneran, his secretary, became an exceptionally caring person. And it was soon obvious she was in love with Peter.

Now tell me, what else does one need to read?

—CHARLES NUETZEL
Thousand Oaks, California
August 2006

//<u>Chapter One</u>\\

Peter Scott looked down at the woman who had just stretched out on the small double bed that was centered in the tiny bedroom of his new apartment.

Joanne Nestor is a beautiful woman, he thought, still puzzled by the fact that he hadn't married her yet. They had been going out together for the last five years, and had known each other for the better part of their lives; yet he had held off going the marriage route. Of course there was the fact of his career to think of. But he couldn't help wondering if this were merely an excuse. He knew it wasn't because of the affair that had continued after their first year of dating. Peter had never been the kind of man who thought just because a woman would go to bed with him that she was written off the list of possible wives. He had never been able to understand that kind of reasoning. When a woman gave her body and love to a man it was a beautiful and valuable gift. She didn't become a slut or tramp because of that. Yet, strangely, even though they had talked about it, and more or less accepted marriage as a future fact, he had always held off.

His eyes moved along her cute, bouncy body.

Her breasts were high, full, with nicely shaped pink points; there was nothing coarse or cheap about her breasts, they had a beauty and class about them, a sensual perfection that always created an emotional, as well as sexual, reaction in him. Her hips were rounded, her stomach while not quite flat was smooth and creamy, soft to kiss and caress. As for her legs, he mused, they were nice, firm, and youthful. Joanne Nestor was a small, full-bodied package of womanhood that could invite the stares of any casual male passerby. In a tight sweater and skirt, her body attracted more than casual stares.

Yes, Peter thought, *Joanne was one hell of an attractive woman whom a man could be proud of having as is own.*

Then why hadn't he pushed for marriage?

Slowly he undressed, keeping his eyes on the nude body of the woman, all the time letting the flooding rush of desire ache up through every nerve.

They had been out for dinner and then gone to the *Tropic Club* for drinks and dancing. It was a celebration because of the job that he had landed that afternoon with Lancer Advertisement Inc. It would be his first honest job, even though he had been working since he was eighteen—but that didn't count, since it was for his father's store. His father, Ross Scott, had always wanted him to learn the business from the ground up and then take over the store. But, after five years of "learning," Peter knew one thing for sure: he wasn't happy working for his father, he wasn't happy with a store; and beyond that, he wanted to make his own way—get to the top with his own ability and intelligence, in a business where he had no personal contact with the boss and owner, where he would have to compete with others for advancement. His father was convinced that he was merely running, afraid to face adult responsibilities; that he didn't have the guts to start something and stick to it. And, worse of all, claimed this was the same reason he was holding off marriage to Joanne. Yet, he reasoned, he had been staying with Jo all these years, even letting himself believe they were a couple deeply in love. Still something was missing.

His attention focused on the woman as he stepped to the bed and sat down beside her. How could a guy not love her; she was lovely, seductive, a great sex partner. Yet why should he want to be with other women, when he had this lovely creature? Why wasn't she enough?

He examined her pert little up-swept nose, ran his fingers through the long waves of her brown hair, then gazed into her deep blue eyes, seeing the reflection of his own emotions and desires there.

There never was any hurry between them, not since that first time, when they had frantically, insanely, made love in the back seat of his car. A madness had possessed both of them, then. But that was understandable since it was the first time for each of them. Since then, Peter had slept with a couple of other women, but never found any who could create the same emotional reaction Joanne fired up in him. As for Joanne, he was certain that she'd never been with another man. To her, the beginning of the affair was the sealing of their love, their complete and final love, forever. She was that kind of woman: a one-man woman. He dreaded the thought of what would happen if she ever learned that he had made love to other girls. The hurt to her would be too much to bear. Even if it were true that the other relationships had been casual, one time only, stands. But if Jo was his soul mate, shouldn't that be enough? Or was it natural for a man to make it with many women, while the woman favored only one partner? Somehow that just didn't make sense.

"Peter," Joanne said in a small, hesitant, worried voice, "are you sure about this job? I mean, really sure?"

"Never been surer about anything else in my life, Jo," he said, caressing her shoulder with the tips of his fingers.

A tremor moved along her arm. "I just don't understand! You had everything all set up. Nothing to worry about; a good income—more then you'll make at the...new job. It just doesn't make sense. What do you want?"

"We've been through all that, Jo. Do we have to?" he asked, irritated.

For a moment she was silent, frowning, her lips pouted in thought, then finally, she slowly smiled, her eyes softened as they looked into his.

"I'll never understand you...in that way. But maybe it's not important. After all, a girl wants to know that the man she loves is sure of himself—just so he makes enough money—I guess it's not important..." Her voice faded out and then she turned away, looking out the side window of the bedroom.

Peter watched the rising and falling of her breasts, feeling the need to kiss and caress them.

"Peter, make love to me. I don't want to think!" Joanne announced, facing him again, sliding her arms up around his neck, gently urging him down to the

10

fullness of her half parted lips.

He let himself be smothered into her, totally escaping any thoughts other than awareness of the texture of her flesh, her lovely skin, and the trembling that raced through her as he traced kisses and caresses along her body. It was like so many times before; easy to fall under the erotic spell of her, even lingering in the lush pleasure of it all, yet at the same time it was, in some ways, almost a detached experience. A part of him was always hungering for something else, something that wasn't there between them. Something was always missing. Not in her kisses, not in her caresses, which raced over him as furiously as his move over her flesh. They simply devoured one another in a well-practiced ritual that climaxed in mutual orgasm, almost always timed to trigger off together. It was nice being with her; but nothing more.

Why, he had never been able to understand. She had been his woman for so long; and they planned on getting married.

Afterwards, a long time afterwards, after the sea calmed down, becoming placid and smooth, after the exhaustion had spent itself out, he heard Joanne slowly slip off the bed and walk out of the room. He waited for her return, thinking about the loveliness of their relationship, the beautiful emotional completion that he always experienced after making love to Joanne. And in his thoughts he again wondered why he hadn't married her; why he was always holding off, as if afraid to take the final plunge that would join their bodies and souls for life.

Maybe it was merely the fear of all men to take that final plunge, he didn't know. But he tried to convince himself of that.

When Joanne returned, she slipped down onto the bed next to him, resting her shoulders and head on the back of the bed. She lighted a cigarette, reached over and placed it between his lips and then lighted another. It was one of those rituals that she seemed to delight in. Normally, when they were out, Joanne was very demanding in expecting him to be the perfect gentleman, and he had always liked that. To him, a woman was to be respected, loved, and served. But after they had experienced a perfect union, Joanne had her own ways of silently thanking him; and this was one of them

They were silent for a long time, until the cigarettes had been finished. Then Joanne leaned over and kissed his lips. That was her other way of thanking him.

She smiled down at Peter and then after a moment, leaned back against the back of the bed again.

"What kind of man is this Ed Beckerman?" she inquired, reaching for another cigarette and lighting it for herself.

"I don't know, really. Seems like a nice sort," Peter said, sitting up, taking her free left hand in his. "Good looking enough. About thirty-eight or -nine, I'd guess. Still in good shape...a little of a stomach showing—but I have an idea he's a real hellion with the women."

"Single?" she inquired in one of those slightly frightened feminine voices that says she is afraid that the man might be a bad influence on her own man.

"Married, I believe."

"Oh," she sighed. That one word said all there was

to say on the subject: fear, dislike, resignation.

"You don't have anything to worry about," Peter assured her, squeezing her hand.

"I better not!" Joanne laughed.

"Well, don't worry. He might be my boss, but that doesn't mean I'm about to do everything he tells me."

"What kind of job is it, really?" Joanne inquired, looking evenly into his eyes.

"Sorta salesman and promoter...well, that's not quite right I'll be expected to be a contact man with clients...something like that. Tomorrow I'll be filled in on all the details. Beckerman said that if I work out there will be fast raises. He believes in rewarding hard workers. At least I'll have that much on my side."

Joanne was silent for a moment, then said:

"I'm worried, Peter. I can't help it."

"Why?"

"Well, you know. You've...well, always driven yourself. You can be...well, pretty driving, I mean...oh, hell, I'm not sure what I mean."

Guiltily he thought about Beckerman's sister-in-law, who happened to walk into the office that day, when Peter was having his interview. He hardly remembered what the conversation was all about between Beckerman and Paula Martin. It had been impossible to ignore the woman.

Yes, he thought, *Paula was the kind of woman who would walk into a room and demand the full attention of all men. It was impossible to look at her without instantly wondering what she must be like in bed—and desiring that lush, exciting body.*

Paula was different from Joanne in that she would attract attention no matter how she was dressed.

Joanne needed tight sweaters and skirts, or something low cut and revealing. Paula could be dressed in a sack and every man would feel the sexual energy generating from her lush, large body. It was impossible to look at the woman and not feel the strength of the animal charm. And when she turned her eyes on you, you felt a full electrical wave slash at you, as if somebody had connected your body to a wall socket.

He shuddered at the thought of ever being trapped with Paula when she turned on the animal call. She was just the kind of woman who could overpower any man she wanted to.

Peter guiltily admitted to himself that it wouldn't be hard to desire a tumble with Paula. He would just about give anything to slip away with her, experience a long, lovely, romantic interlude. Her image had haunted him for hours. Even now, after having been so intimate with Joanne, he felt a rush of pleasure just thinking about Paula.

Angrily he attempted to turn his thoughts away from the woman. He tried to turn his attention toward Joanne Nestor who was so lovely, so seductively nude, next to him. The woman he loved; the woman he planned on marrying.

As their eyes met, Peter had the terrible feeling that she was reading his thoughts. But, of course, that was impossible.

And, anyway, Paula wasn't about to play intimate games with him. It was merely natural for a man to have an automatic reaction toward the sexual package like Paula.

He forced himself to accept that reasoning and was able to, for the time, put Paula out of his mind.

Again he forced his attention toward Joanne.

She smiled, then after a moment asked: "Peter how long do we have to wait?"

The question was an old one and needed no more explanation than that.

He shrugged. "Let me have a chance to get settled on this job."

"I think you're just afraid of getting married!" she accused, annoyed. "You can't be a little boy all your life!"

Then her lips were wide, offering themselves, silent.

He kissed her, passionately, his tongue plunging deep into the cavity of her mouth. She closed her lips around the kiss and then squirmed hungrily against him.

It was a long time before they broke from the embrace and by that time neither were in the mood for conversation anymore.

During the night, Peter woke, sweating. For a long time he lay in the darkness, trying to calm his nerves down. The dream had been about his father. One of those horrible nightmares that had reflected reality too vividly. Like in reality, there had been the scene, the fight, which had centered around him, around his driving urge to find himself. And, like reality, his father had screamed: "You're nothing but a bum! That's what. You have everything you could need. You're just lazy, afraid to face life, to face yourself and responsibilities. You're running. And how long will you last in this...little job? Just how long? How long? Until it gets boring! Look at the way you've treated Jo...holding her off, and off. You should be married, settled down. But you're afraid...gutless." On and on like that until he'd awakened.

It was a long, long time before sleep returned. And during that time, Peter couldn't help wondering why he had dreamed about his father's words. Could they be true?

//**Chapter Two**\\

Paula Martin sat out in the patio of her sister's large home, smoking, furious, thinking about herself and life, and men. Always men. But especially what Ed had just done!

Damn him! She thought, bitterly.

Ed Beckerman, her brother-in-law, had been quite drunk during the party that was only now slowly coming to a painful end. She had always been aware of his interest in her; it couldn't be ignored. His eyes had peeled her clothing off more than once. In a way it was flattering. To many women it was delightful to know that the men around her can't help desiring to take her to bed. To Paula it was almost an obsession. The need to have men want her was all embracing. She couldn't be in the same room with a man without attempting to make him want her. But with Ed, that was something different.

Regardless of all her faults, and Paula had admitted them to herself a long time before, she didn't like the idea of sleeping with her sister's husband. She loved Diana. She loved her too much to do anything that might harm or hurt her. It didn't matter to Paula that she felt a sharp, automatic attraction toward Ed Beckerman. Any woman would find him attractive. It

17

was nothing more than that. In fact, she had spent many long, lonely nights thinking about what it might be like with her brother-in-law; but those were casual, innocent thoughts, since they weren't coupled with actions. She had never once done anything to even intimate flirtation toward Ed. He was, in fact, the only man she had never even made the slightest hint of a flirtation. As far as she was concerned he was no less than a brother to her.

But less than twenty minutes before, when she was in the den, alone, fixing herself a drink, Ed Beckerman walked in, closed the door behind him and then stepped up to her, a fiery flicker in his brown eyes. He had come to a stop only inches away from Paula, and his eyes had dipped to the low cut neckline, almost absorbing her fleshy breasts.

Then suddenly Ed had leaned over, and before she could do anything to stop him, his lips fell against the crevice between her hefty breasts.

That was as far as he got. She jerked back, away from him. "For God's sake, Ed, what the damned hell are you doing?" she snapped angrily, confused, startled.

For a stunned moment neither of them said anything, then Ed grinned crookedly, took a step toward her.

"You know I've wanted you for a long time, Paula," he said, still grinning.

"Lay off, Ed! No dice! I'm surprised at you." He came to a stop. Frowned. "What's wrong, Paula. I know about you...there's no secret that you'll lay anything with pants on! Hell, what's wrong with me?"

"You should know!" Paula announced picking up

a pack of cigarettes from the small home bar and lighting it, simply because she didn't know anything else to do to keep herself calmed down.

"Why should that bother you? I know you gave it out to Lloyd Campbell, and he's as married as they come! Three kids and—"

"That was different. He was cuffing into any girl willing to give it to him!" she snapped back, glaring at Ed.

Ed grinned again. "What if I was like him?"

"You better not let me know about it!" she warned.

"I don't think there's any harm. Surely you know that I've played around!" Ed told her, pouring himself a drink, all the time his eyes flicking back to her exposed neckline.

"What the hell brought this on?" Paula demanded, taking a drag of her cigarette.

"You know...or you should...knowing your sister. A man...a man needs a woman...a real woman! You're a real woman and—"

"Stop it right now, Ed. You're drunk. That's what's wrong with you! Now stop it before things get too involved!" Paula snapped angrily, savagely hitting the bar with her fist. "I don't want to hear another word from you about this. I'm off limits to you—and that's that!"

She turned and started out of the room, but the man came hurriedly after her, grabbed her shoulder and twisted her brutally around. Then, without knowing how it happened, Ed yanked her into his arms and their lips were blended together in a hot kiss. Automatically her mouth had opened. It was an instinctive reaction for Paula. She felt the man's tongue fire deep into her mouth as he crushed her against his body. For a moment she was breathless, almost overpowered by the wild erotic pleasure of the kiss. Then she struggled to get free of Ed. Strangely he released her, but there was an odd, pleased expression on his rugged face.

Angrily, Paula had rushed out of the room and gone out onto the patio to sit down, to cool off the seething rage burning through her mind and body.

Men had always been a major factor in her life; and intimate relations had started early on, in her teenage.

She was now twenty-six years old, but her experience with men was that of a woman twice that age. It had started a long time ago, when she had developed young for her age. She and her sister, Diana, had been born and raised in a small town, where everybody knew everybody else. As a young girl, Paula had played with boys rather than other girls. Girl's games had always been dull and uninteresting. She had never been interested in dolls; and as a woman she had little interest in children.

When Paula turned fourteen, her breasts had already begun to develop into eye-catching fullness— even though they had a long way to go before they would be the full, large shapes that she now so proudly displayed. At fifteen she discovered there was something more to playing with boys that met the eye. An older boy, Dave Turner, who lived down the block from Paula's home, had started dating her a little after her fifteenth birthday, and his idea of a date involved a lot of kissing and finally a lot of petting. Paula didn't really know what it was all about.

Her parents were of the old style, who believed

that sex wasn't a topic of conversation, even between themselves. Paula had many times wondered, in the years that followed, just what kind of sex life her father must have had with Silvia Martin. From what she had learned in her twenty-six years, Paula was certain that her mother hadn't liked sex—that her mother was like Diana, cold, frigid. Paula had favored her father, both in body structure and apparently in physical hungers.

That one night, some weeks after starting to date Dave Turner, when they were in the back seat of his car, and his hands had become a little more exploratory, Paula had discovered a weakness and excitement that she'd never before experienced. Having no real education in sex, she had not the least idea of what was happening, or what could have happened because of what the boy did to her. When his hand became too friendly, searching lower over her body and finally reaching up under her skirt, Paula had gone wild and had been willing to do anything he asked. After that night, Paula found herself needing more of the same. David had been tickled to death.

And as time continued, she discovered that other boys took a strangely intense interest in her. Dates were fast and then one night, when she came home a little later than usual, her father had taken her aside and told her a few things about life that were down right frightening. She never told her dad she'd been letting boys do "that" to her; but she did stop until after her eighteenth birthday, at which time she learned from other girls in college that there were ways to take care of herself, to protect herself from complications. It wasn't easy for a single girl to get the required devices to protect herself; but in short time, through some girl friends, Paula managed to find a doctor who was willing, for a good price, to help her out.

Then she'd become involved with a young man who was studying to become a lawyer. She fell in love for the first and last time in her life. The affair had raged for several months at college, and then, during the summer vacation she received a letter from Vern that he was engaged to get married to a home town girl; and reading between the lines she guessed that he'd gotten some girl in trouble and was doing the right thing by marrying her. It had hurt Paula, and for a long time she didn't want anything to do with men.

Now things were different. And she sat there considering her surroundings; her sister's home; her sister's "universe"! The party.

She knew that her sister Diana was cold, that Ed was sleeping out with other women, she had known that for some time. But this was the first time it had come out in the open between Ed and herself; the first time he had made a pass. And she hoped with all her heart the last time he ever made a pass at her.

Paula suddenly remembered the man in Ed's office.

That was a good-looking bastard, she thought, smiling. He'd almost eaten her up with his eyes.

She tried to think of his name, but couldn't remember. They had been casually and politely introduced, but the name had gone in one ear and out the other. That was something new for, Paula. Usually she remembered names pretty good; especially good-looking men's names. And this guy was one hell of a hunk of man.

Jet back hair, tall, broad shouldered. There had been a sensitive look about his gray-blue eyes that had intrigued Paula. It had been fun flirting with him. The way he'd really given her the once over. Her nerves had tingled, her breasts had fired with hard needles. It had been an exciting game they had played.

She remembered promising herself that she would make it a point to see this guy again. Then had forgotten all about it.

Now, sitting on the patio, Paula made the promise again, this time really impressing her mind.

She puzzled over the fact that she couldn't remember his name. That was very annoying to Paula. She had always prided herself in remembering names. Why had his slipped her mind? Had his effect been that strong on her?

She shrugged and then slowly stood, looked at the large, U-shaped house and then sighing, started for the living room. There she would be safe from any more advances, now that her nerves had settled.

* * * * * * *

Diana Beckerman felt a sense of uneasiness as she stepped from the children's room and headed toward her bedroom. She knew that Ed would be coming to her, to her room, to her bed, wanting to make love. It was a pattern that always went into effect when he'd had too much to drink—and that was usually the night of the weekly party.

She pulled off her bra and examined her breasts more carefully, almost angrily.

Why couldn't she like sex the way her sister did? It

had never been a very rewarding situation for her. Only that one time—with her roommate in college. But she didn't like to think about that—she never did think about it more than a second. Shame and disgust would cut through Diana every time she remembered that one night with the other woman.

She tore her thoughts away from that night, and looked away from the mirror.

Slipping out of her panties, Diana stepped into the private half-bath and turned on the shower, waited until the water was warm enough, and then stepped under the spray.

Some time later she turned off the water and then dried herself. Then, taking her time, Diana creamed her face, taking off the little makeup that was her habit of wearing, then applied cold cream, carefully, over every inch of her face. Maybe that would stop Ed, she told herself hopefully.

Finally, Diana opened the bathroom door and stepped out into the bedroom.

She stopped cold and instinctively attempted to cover her nakedness.

Ed Beckerman was lying on her bed, naked, looking at her.

"What you doing here?" she fairly cried, defensively.

He merely grinned and waited, his eyes running over her body. There wasn't any wild passion in his gaze, but merely a strangely glazed, drunken look.

"Do we have to?" Diana pleaded, reaching for a robe that was draped over her vanity chair. She pulled it tightly around her body.

He didn't answer her.

Diana frantically attempted to think of something to say or do that would make it impossible for her husband to demand her body. Actually, she didn't have any right to deny him; that much she was willing to admit. But the idea of submitting was almost disgusting to her.

Sighing, she finally stepped to the bed and lay down, on the far side, away from her husband.

The man turned, slipped close and then crudely opened the robe. His large hand cupped one of her breasts, then he slipped down and kissed it, his mustache tickling in an annoying way.

Diana tensed and decided it was useless to fight. Ed wasn't in the mood to be turned down. She could tell by the direct, demanding approach he had made toward her.

She lay back and let her husband have his way with her body. Several times during his activities she felt a light edge of desire start to worry itself through her and then it would fade away, disappear as he suddenly would change his direction, as he would move on to some other portion of her body.

Oh, if he could only make her enjoy what he was doing! If only once he could give her the pleasure that should be hers. But never! Never had it really ended in complete satisfaction. Ever since that first time, on their marriage night, it had been an exhausting painful experience for Diana. She loved her husband and she loved her children—if it weren't for that, Diana might have ended the marriage.

Finally the man moved down bodily to her and she felt the weight of him become a part of her.

She tensed, fighting against the urge to scream.

Every thrust of him against her was almost brutal, and felt even angry. Then a light, mild sensation of pleasure ebbed through her and then faded away as the man lifted and fell to her side.

She lay there for a long time, wanting to cry, wanting to scream, to do anything other than merely lay there quietly waiting for him to leave for his own bedroom and leave her alone in her misery.

If she could only be more like her sister—at least to the extent where she could enjoy it. But she wasn't.

* * * * * * *

The man lay there bathed in his own depressed thought, angry at what had happened a few moments before. He had taken his wife because he needed some outlet, some escape from his thoughts. It was always that way. He made love to Diana with an automatic detachment. She was a woman, a body, which would yield to him on demand. But she wasn't anything exciting. She merely lay there, stony, waiting for him to finish. It had been like that right from the beginning. At first he had believed it would be possible to teach her, to, in time, develop a passion in her supple body; but instead it had merely gotten worse, until now he only took her when there wasn't anything else to do— when another woman wasn't around to give him a really charged session.

Guilt ate at him because of what had happened between Paula and himself earlier that evening. He hadn't wanted it to happen, but there it was. He had been drunk and desperate. Paula was such a package of sexual energy. She was completely the opposite of

Diana. If only his wife were like that, everything would be perfect.

He knew that in time, some day, if Paula kept being around, he would have to have her. It was becoming an obsession with him. It wasn't easy to have such a sister-in-law, knowing that she took on with any stud willing to grab her body. It was damned hard under any circumstances, but especially when the wife was cold ice.

Ed shrugged off the thoughts, angrily sat up, flung his legs over the edge of the bed and for a moment turned and looked at Diana's reposed body.

Damned if he didn't love her. And damned if he didn't feel guilty and like a beast every time he made love to her. He knew that Diana only gave in because she thought it was her wifely duty. If only women knew what that did to a man. It ate out his guts night and day.

Yes, a man wanted a woman who desired him, who liked sex, who gave because she desired, and not because it was her duty.

He turned away from his wife and walked out of the room, sick inside, defeated by the way things had worked out in his private life. As a business executive, he was a success; as a husband-lover he fizzled, because his wife was frigid and cold.

If only he could talk about sex with his wife; but she was all too much like her mother had been. She wasn't anything like Paula at all. The two sides of the same coin—and he married the wrong side— regardless of the fact that Paula didn't seem to be the marrying kind. No man could satisfy her for very long.

He stepped into his own room and then slipped

into bed, turning out the bed-lamp.

Ed Beckerman lay there for a long time thinking about his life, thinking about all the women he had made.

At eighteen he had learned the facts of life from a nympho who couldn't get enough men to satisfy the burn of her body. It had been a bad first experience from that point of view, for very few women were that savagely demanding. In college he had learned about love and sex, and then about heartbreak. Later he met his future wife and had fallen madly in love with her from the first moment. Why, he had never known for sure. That first date, when he attempted the normal forward passes, she blocked them, firmly, even politely. That's when he learned that Diana wasn't the kind of girl to put out on the first or last date, until the wedding ring had been put on her finger. From then on he had really been sunk. They married a few months later, and then the first night had proven a shattering experience from which they had never really gotten over. In the beginning he had never thought about stepping out on Diana. He loved her far too much, and if their sexual lives weren't what they should be, at least she gave in to his advances; and after all, he told himself so many times that he'd lost count, sex wasn't the whole bit. Now Ed realized that while sex wasn't the complete thing, a marriage wasn't complete without a normal sexual relationship. If a man didn't get it at home, in time he would go out and find it somewhere else.

Finally, he managed to relax his body, his nerves and muscles and then press a blanket of gray over his thoughts. Then sleep settled down, giving him rest from the tormented reality of life.

//<u>Chapter Three</u>\\

Ann Fenneran looked at her new boss, Peter Scott. She couldn't help admiring his powerful looking frame, his broad shoulders. There was an intense expression in his eyes when he stared off into the distant in thought. They had been introduced only an hour before by Ed Beckerman. It was a quick, hurried introduction. "Miss Fenneran, this is Pete Scott. I'll want you to show him the ropes and for a while try to carry the ball as much as possible for him, until he gets his feet on the ground! Okay, honey?"

Then Beckerman had left them alone. A short, polite conversation had followed in which Peter Scott had asked the normal run of the mill questions about herself.

"Been working here long?"

"Yes, about three years."

"You look too young to be working that long.

"Live alone?"

"None of your business," she had snapped back, embarrassed suddenly and not knowing why.

"I'm sorry. It isn't really. Just popped out." His face looked confused for a moment and she suddenly felt sorry for him.

"I live alone," she told him in a small voice. "I

30

wanted to be independent. And so I am, I guess." Her last remark had sounded bitter even to her own ears.

But he didn't say anything about that.

"Well, we might as well get started. Just, exactly, what is it that I'll be doing?" He smiled almost boyishly. Then added: "Actually, the only thing I know is that I'm supposed to see clients and try to get them to let us do their work for them."

Ann smiled half professionally and half friendly, said: "Well, actually, you'll be talking to executives from industry, but in the beginning with Mr. Beckerman. You'll listen, I'll be there to take notes for you, and just follow up anything that Beckerman says. In the first weeks, at least, you'll be really only learning the ropes. After a meeting it is our job to put together a complete report for Beckerman. That is, a transcription of any meetings, together with any contracts, agreements, or verbal messages from the client in question. You'll be a go-between for Mr. Beckerman in the beginning months. Once you learn your way around, you'll be put in charge of some clients' accounts—but until then you're not much more than a figurehead of this office.

"Thanks," he had said, grinning and standing, coming to her side, looking down into her eyes. It had been the only real close moment since they met. There was a strangely offbeat feeling of flirtation, without any real out and out overtures. Just a "thank you" expression in his eyes as they met hers.

Now, Peter was looking through some of the material she had gotten from the files on the Kelbore Company. And she was finding it hard to keep from examining every detail of his handsome face. Her eyes had hesitated more than once at his lips, which were nicely shaped, neither thin nor large. They had a mannishness to them that attracted her.

During the last few years, Ann had gone through several affairs. In the beginning, when she was only twenty, Ann had believed that sex should be saved for marriage. It wasn't that her parents had been closed minded, and had, in fact, been quite liberal minded and open about talking things over with her. But more than that she had hoped for the most romantic perfection with the man she married. At the time, Ann couldn't imagine a more romantic situation other than falling in love, getting married and giving herself to the one and only man she loved on the wedding night. Then she had met Tom, and things had gone out the window. He had an apartment all his own, and his line, his good looks, and his overwhelming animal attractiveness had finally, after six months, overcome her reluctance. She was in love, and he seemed to have been in love with her.

That first night, on the couch, when he pulled her into his arms had driven her beyond the point of control. She merely remembered all the things he had told her about love, about the relationship of man and woman, about getting sex out of the way before marriage, before it was possible to make a mistake just because both parties wanted to make love to each other. He had been so right about that. Up to that point Ann had believed that she was really in love with Tom, and that there could never be any other for her. In fact, it turned out that she merely had that driving sexual desire for him, and once it had been satisfied, she was able to look at their relationship in a more unemotional way. In time, a little over two months, the affair had simmered out.

Ann just thanked God that her parents were intelligent enough and wise enough to understand a few facts about life. It wasn't often that a child was blessed with such parents. Actually she couldn't help believing that they might have had an affair before they were married. She knew, for a fact, that her father had been living with a woman before he met her mother.

Ann returned her thoughts to the present and the man before her. "Is there anything more you might want, Mr. Scott?"

He looked up, smiled. "Let's not be formal between ourselves. If the company requires last names in front of clients, that's one thing...but between us...can't we make it Peter and Ann?"

She grinned and nodded. "Okay, Peter."

"Thanks, Ann," he said, lowering his eyes to the papers in front of him, as she turned and walked out of the room.

* * * * * * *

A couple of hours later, Peter was giving his eyes some rest after having read a number reports on the Kelbore Company. His eyes burned and he was already exhausted from the combination of reading and the aftermath of his celebration the night before with Joanne. He thought about Joanne for a moment and then found his thoughts shifting to Ann Fenneran. She seemed like a nice young woman. At least he would be having an attractive, hard-working, intelligent secretary at his side. That was a relief.

The buzzer at his desk jarred the silence and for a moment he was electrified. His thoughts had been so completely introspected that the reality which surrounded him had slipped away into a meaningless blur.

Peter jerked to attention, leaned across the desk, pushed a button and then said: "Yes?"

Ann Fenneran's voice said, in a strangely formal and stiff manner: "There's a Miss Martin to see you, Mr. Scott."

For a moment he couldn't imagine who Miss Martin was. Then suddenly, like a jarring slap across the face, he remembered. All at once he was shaking and not knowing why. Then a second reaction set in.

What the hell did she want? Did she work for the firm? He hadn't known that.

"Mr. Scott, are you still there?" Ann's voice inquired, worried sounding.

"Yes...yes. Let her come in," he said, puzzled, releasing the switch and leaning back in his swivel chair.

He tried to calm his thoughts, tried to prepare himself for the next moments.

Then the door opened and Paula Martin stepped into the office, dressed like a jungle cat looking frantically for a mate.

She closed the door behind her and then stepped seductively forward, smiling.

"Hello...Mr. Scott," she greeted, standing in front of the large oak desk, like some Goddess of Passion who has come out of the heavenly domain to torment mortal humans to their doom.

She was decked out in a slinky green dress that accented the cat green of her smoldering eyes. The top of the dress opened wide around her throat and dipped low enough to give an excellent view of large, thrust-ing breasts. Her hands were covered with small white gloves and she was carrying a white purse. There was a style about her that seemed classy while at the same time like a jungle tigress, hunting for the inevitable mate. Her eyes flashed as they met his, almost too boldly, too brazen, both flirtatious and amused.

For a choking moment he didn't know what to do or say. His mind kept saying over and over again: *why the hell was she here?*

What could she want with him? He couldn't help guessing.

For an awkward silence, which seemed to stretch out for eternity, she gazed at him. There was nothing, really, which indicated what he felt was the obvious—that she was making a play for him.

A tremor rushed over Peter as he thought about the idea of folding that tall, large, voluptuous body against his.

Finally he said: "Well, what can I do for you?"

"Mind if I sit down?" she inquired, looking at the chair next to her, in front of the desk.

"No...of course. I'm sorry!" He half stood, awk-wardly.

Paula grinned. It was the kind of action that had all the sexual energy of a naked girl doing an erotic dance. She moistened the surface of her mouth with the delicate point of her tongue. Her eyes lowered slightly for a moment, as if she were unsure of herself.

"Well...well...I came here to ask about a job!" she suddenly blurted out. Her eyes didn't meet his.

It took Peter a full minute to collect his thoughts, to organize himself to that statement. In the first place he knew she was lying, because he wasn't the guy she would come to in order to get a job. That was Beckerman's business—plus the fact she was the man's sister-in-law.

"Well, Miss Martin—"

"Paula?" she offered, meeting his eyes with a level gaze that revealed nothing.

"Paula. I don't know anything about that. I just started to work." He hesitated and decided to come right out and tell her what he was thinking. "And I believe you know that!"

She smiled, slowly. "It could be true, you know. After all, I am Ed's sister in-law, and a woman would like to know she could get a job regardless...or rather...on her own hook!" But the smile mocked him knowingly.

"But wouldn't you go to Personnel?" he suggested blandly, trying to control the automatic reaction which was slowly ebbing through his body.

"Yes...but what if I wanted to meet a young, new executive? What would you do?" she countered, challenging him with her eyes.

The sudden change of direction of her approach was startling. A shiver raced down his spine. He didn't know what to say to that. In fact, there was little that he could say to such a direct approach.

"What would you do, Peter Scott?" she inquired in a very low, sensual voice.

Peter shrugged, took a drag of his cigarette and then nervously stubbed it out, still only half smoked.

"Well, to be honest, Peter," she said, caressing his name with her voice, "I'm not the kind of girl to play games. Just that when I came in here I got a little...well, overwhelmed and...believe it or not," which he didn't, "I was a little embarrassed and afraid to come right out and well, you know." The shrug of her shoulders bounced her breasts suggesting that she didn't wear a bra. The idea more than intrigued.

He forced himself to play it cool. "Look, I don't know what you have in mind," he said in an almost irritated voice, "but I am trying to do a job and..."

"I could be of help to you," she suggested boldly.

"I guess you could," he smiled.

"Well, I wasn't really offering that! But...I guess you must think me horrible. Women just don't go out and...well, throw themselves at men." She laughed almost nervously. Taking another cigarette, she lighted it, all the time her eyes holding to his. "It's just that when I want something...I have to do something about it. I've always been a little direct, you know."

"No, I don't."

"You will learn, won't you? Dinner and cocktails, tonight?" she suggested invitingly, blowing smoke in his direction.

"Have an engagement."

"Before or after my suggestion?" she inquired bitingly, her eyes flaring with emotion.

"Both...before and after," he told her seriously.

"Lunch, then. Surely there's nothing you can be tied up with then. And it is lunchtime, and I am starved—and thirsty. Can't do without a good Martini before lunch. I think a Martini sets off the meal, don't you?" she asked conversationally, her voice revealing her complete confidence of his acceptance for the luncheon date.

"Okay," Peter said. "But I can't get over your approach."

She laughed, throatily. "I'll admit it was a bit forward. I'm sorry. But I don't know of any better way to let a man know that I'm interested. If I'd waited for the right moment to come along...that might have been ages. And I'm not the kind of woman who likes to wait."

He could well imagine that. Lovely beyond words, sexy as Hell itself, and probably so damned spoiled when it came to men that she wasn't afraid to demand what she wanted.

"I must say," Peter told her, standing, "that it's quite flattering to have such a lovely woman, well...make her interest so quickly known and—"

"And come right out and ask for a date?" she offered, amused, controlled, sure of herself.

"And come right out and ask for a date," he admitted, stepping around the desk and coming to her side. For a moment he was almost afraid to touch her. The mere idea was just too much.

It was Paula who settled that issue. She reached out and tucked her hand under his left arm. And in such a manner they left the office, walked past Ann Fenneran's desk and out into the hallway outside the office.

* * * * * * *

Ann Fenneran sat there, stunned. Ever since Paula Martin had come into the office she had felt a tingling jealous anger.

She knew Paula's reputation, and like most women, was frightened of the out and out sensual attractiveness of her. Paula slipped into bed with any man who looked promising; she was famous for taking up with every new executive who came to work for Lancer. But this was some kind of record.

Ann sat there, angry and puzzled over her anger.

//<u>Chapter Four</u>\\

Paula Martin watched the man as he ordered Martinis. He had taken them to a nicely atmospheric restaurant that had low lighting and quiet service. As the waiter left and Peter turned his eyes in her direction, she felt a shock wave of excitement.

He was a damned handsome brute, she thought, still mystified by her actions that had brought her to this point with a total stranger.

In his office she had actually become confused, and still felt she'd made a bloody fool of herself. But all was well that ended well, and the only thing that actually mattered was that she was sitting across from him in the booth of a nice flashy restaurant, waiting for cocktails.

Paula laughed. "You don't have to be afraid of me."

"Why not?"

"Why should you?"

"How do I know the boss hasn't put you on my...sent you to feel me out?"

She merely smiled, said: "Then he would have made things a lot more easy for me. I wouldn't have had to make a damned fool of myself, would I?"

"Why did you make it hard?" he inquired. "Why

not have Ed Beckerman introduce us?"

Paula shuddered mentally at the thought. "There are personal reasons."

"What makes a girl like you...well...interested in a guy like me?" Peter inquired.

She didn't get a chance to answer that question right away, and was glad. The drinks came then, and they both picked up their cocktails and sipped. She had a chance to think out her answer more carefully. When it was necessary to answer it, she said: "Why shouldn't a girl be attracted to a good looking man?"

"I guess there's no reason...but—"

"But they don't come right out and lay it on the line?"

Peter laughed. "I guess so."

"Let's talk about something else."

"Okay. About you?"

"What's there to tell?"

"Well, start with what you do for a living."

"I have a little money," Paula admitted, not adding that most of it came from boyfriends along the way. It wasn't hard for an attractive woman to manage without working, if she were willing to throw around a little playtime. She threw around a lot. Between that and her modeling, she managed pretty nicely. "I do a little modeling now and then."

"What kind?"

"Fashion shows."

"I bet you make a mint," he grinned, eyeing her figure.

"Actually, to be honest, I'm limited to sexy things. Bathing suits are good."

"I bet." He was silent for a moment then asked:

"What about this topless bathing suit?" His eyes gleamed as if he were mentally picturing her with one on.

"The new and coming thing."

"Think it will really catch on?"

"Didn't the bikini? It took time. First in private homes, pools, then on the beaches. Some women like to show off."

"And you?"

"I don't think it's necessary," she admitted.

"Meaning?" he pushed, an amused expression gleaming in his gray blue eyes.

"Meaning that a woman who is sure of herself doesn't have to go around with a topless bathing suit. She gets enough stares. Anyway, what you can't see is sometimes even more sexy than what you can see."

"Sometimes," he admitted, taking a sip of his Martini. His eyes hesitated on her neckline. They talked generally about nothing of importance, merely polite conversation to gap the dull less inspired moments between sips of Martini and cigarettes.

Paula was certain that Peter Scott was the slow, careful lover. His eyes had a sensitive quality about them that suggested the kind of man who considered the woman, who was more concerned about loving her body, giving pleasure to her nerves, rather than merely taking pleasure from her.

When the meal came, a New York steak for Peter, a Liver and Onions for herself, Paula asked:

"Do you really have to keep your date tonight?" He nodded. "Can't break it."

"That important?"

"That important."

"A girl?"

He hesitated, then said: "Yes."

Serious?"

"Has been."

"Sounds promising."

They were silent during the rest of the meal, and not until he was waiting for the check did Paula say: "I've enjoyed myself. I hope we can get together again." She questioned him with her eyes, all the time carefully studying his for reaction.

"It's been fun."

"How about tomorrow night?"

He tensed slightly.

"At my place. I'm an excellent cook, and..."

"I don't know," he told her in a careful voice, as if he were unsure of himself.

"Why not? Cocktails, dinner, wine, dim lights, romantic music," she offered in her most suggestive voice.

His expression weakened slightly. "Let me think about it."

"When will you let me know?"

"You're pushing too hard," he told her almost irritated.

"I'm not pushing...only offering what I want to offer!" she countered defensively.

The waiter came then and Peter paid the bill. As they walked out onto the street and headed toward the building where the Lancer Advertising Company was located, Peter suddenly said, out of a clear sky, "Okay, damn it all. Tomorrow night."

* * * * * * *

As Peter returned to his office he was painfully aware of the strange look that Ann Fenneran gave him and he puzzled over it for a moment before returning his thoughts back to Paula Martin. He was still dazed by what happened.

The rest of the day was a torment of guilty thoughts. He even found it hard to look directly into the eyes of his secretary.

When he left the office, getting into his car in the parking lot, he sat there for a short time, lighting a cigarette and smoking in thoughtful silence. He was supposed to pick Joanne Nestor up at work, where she made her living as a typist for an insurance firm. He almost dreaded facing the woman he had been going out with for so many years. He felt much like a husband who is about to cheat on his wife.

Finally, he started the engine and then headed out of the parking lot.

* * * * * * *

Joanne Nestor could feel it the moment she slipped into the car next to Peter. It was a silent reserve, almost a wall between them. Maybe she had gotten to know Peter so well that she could almost read his thoughts by the expression on his face. She had never known anybody who could reveal so much in a mere glance.

"What's wrong?"

"Oh, nothing. Just that I...well, feel nervous. That's to be expected, I guess," he told her in a distant voice.

They sat in silence for a long time, until he suddenly said: "How about a Mexican dinner?"

"That's fine with me."

Joanne felt suddenly frightened and didn't know why. It was the first time that there had ever been a real wall between them. She had expected Peter to be bubbling over about his job, telling her all sorts of details, none of which she would understand, but she would listen carefully, so that he would feel she wanted to hear everything.

Peter took her to the El Taco, a nicely intimate Mexican restaurant, ordered two Stingers and the combination plate for both of them. There followed a short awkward silent brooding and then Peter began talking, like a record gone wild.

"This is a wonderful job, Jo. I can see the possibilities. They go all the way to the top. You should see the office I have...real plush. Thick carpets, a large oak desk, a big window behind the desk and...well, you'll have to come up one of these days and see it all...but there's no fooling around. They want me to do a lot of extra homework and study. I can understand that. My secretary got some files out on this whiskey account we have...that's the one I'll probably be working on first...and boy you should see it! It'll take me ages just to weed through that file—then I'll only be scratching the surface. You know what they have in mind for me? Taking over accounts and…"

He went on and on, through the cocktails, which were ordered over again and for a third time before the meal was brought. He continued to talk throughout the meal, nervously, rapidly.

And with every moment, Joanne felt more and more frightened. She had never seen him like this before. He was talking too much. Peter normally was more the quiet, thoughtful type. She couldn't help thinking he had something on his mind, something that he was hiding from her.

Immediately she suspected a woman and that knifed at her like acid. All she could think about was the secretary. When he ran down a little she asked: "What kind of secretary do you have?"

"Oh, she's fine. Knows her business. I think we'll be able to work real good together and—"

"Not too good, I hope!" she said much more lightly than she felt.

"Oh, honey, you know there could never be another woman."

That settled it for Joanne. He had been far too convincing in his tone of voice, and he had never called her honey before.

"*Dos combinaciones*," their waiter Miguel said, setting the hot plates down in front of them.

But she was sick throughout the whole meal: sick, nervous, and irritable—and it wasn't the food.

When they returned to the car and Peter suggested they go to some hotel, she knew for certain something was wrong. It was the first time they had ever gone to a hotel in town; usually it was his or her place.

The change, sudden and so complete, in their relationship, was almost too much to adjust to so quickly. She wanted time to think things out, but didn't have it.

All she could think of, as he was getting a room for them in the Hillman Hotel, was: *How could all this happen so quickly—after several years of such closeness?*

Maybe it was merely her imagination, she told herself as he came up to her and said: "Well, Jo..."

Peter took her arm and led the way to the elevator.

They didn't say a thing until he was opening the door to Room 107. It was a room number that Joanne couldn't help feeling she would remember for the rest of her life. In this room, she was almost certain, would be decided the fate of their future relationship.

//<u>Chapter Five</u>\\

Peter felt awkward and uneasy as he closed the door behind him and watched Joanne step across the small, beautifully furnished room. She glided over to the large double windows and pulled open the drapes, looked out over the city below.

"It's a lovely sight, isn't it Peter?" she said over her shoulder.

He leaned down and kissed the back of her neck, running his tongue over the smooth, soft white flesh.

She trembled slightly and worked her head back and forth against the kiss.

After a moment they stepped back, Peter re-closed the drapes and then pulled Joanne into his arms. She melted against him, hungrily, her lips open, and her body eager and wanting.

They kissed, but it somehow seemed different, distant, as if he was somebody else and she was somebody else. Strangely the excitement was gone.

For a few seconds he held the kiss and then pulled away from Joanne.

How beautiful and childlike she is, he thought, pleased and annoyed at the same time. Like an innocent little doe. He was her first lover; she gave herself to him because she really cared, really was in love

48

with him. She had given to him the most beautiful and wonderful gift a woman could offer a man. He couldn't help loving her.

She came into his arms like a little child, bravely and honestly, with all her heart in the action. Her lips moved up under his, almost touching, bright and shiny in the light of the room. Her eyes half lidded, her hands caressed the back of his neck, her hips pressed softly to his. He felt her breasts, breathing hard, hugging to his chest.

So like a little child; an innocent little child who needed protection and love.

The emotion welled through him as he touched her lips with his.

He felt the softness of her mouth as it trembled under his kiss, the moist excitement of it as she parted her lips. Joanne tensed, her fingers hugged around the back of his head, caressed, her hips surged harder to him, almost rotating.

Finally they were cheek to cheek and she was moaning soft words of love in his ear, pleading words that said all too well the desperation of her love for him.

Then as the caressing and kissing became more meaningful, more hotly demanding, he felt the normal animal desire racing the blood faster and faster through him like lava burning away all other sensations other than the burning blistering need that slowly took complete control. And when they blended their bodies together for the last insanity of their lovemaking, Peter had a moment of strangely detached awareness.

Afterward, as he lay next to Joanne on the bed, he felt terrible aching guilt at what had happened. He tried to explain them away, but it did no good. He tried to tell himself that it was merely an accident and that he'd only fully responded to the new pattern of Joanne's lovemaking that had been so much more aggressive than ever before.

Yet the image of Paula simmered between him and Joanne, and he felt the needling tingle of excitement race his nerves wild.

God, what was happening to him? Was he tired of Joanne? Could it be that after their long, intimate affair, he was ready to chuck it all for a quick thrill with a hot bitching tramp? Was it possible that all that had happened between the two of them, all they had shared together, meant really nothing other than an exercise in experience?

He shuddered at the thought and then forced himself to lean over and plant a soft, teasing kiss on Joanne's flesh.

She moved and moaned and then pulled him tighter against her. And after that they made love once more.

But Peter found himself completely detached this time, more than ever before. He wasn't even really thinking about what happened between them, he wasn't really even aware of the effect that the feminine form had on his body. He was a man, and Joanne was a woman, and his body responded to the naked nearness of female flesh—and this time it was nothing more than that. He was thinking about Paula, and actually enjoying it.

* * * * * *

When Peter told her that he couldn't see her that night, Joanne knew instinctively that something was really happening between the two of them which would have lasting effects on their relationship—the kind of effects that she dreaded the most. A fear that it was ending couldn't be ignored.

They were sitting in the car, outside her apartment. It was still dark outside, since they had gotten up at five, quickly dressed, had a short breakfast in the hotel coffee shop and then driven to her home.

For a moment she had the impulse to ask him why he would be too busy, but one look into his eyes and she knew it was no use. A sinking feeling flushed over her as she leaned close and kissed him.

"I'll see you tomorrow, then?" she offered, almost frightened of the answer.

"Probably," he said casually. "Call you."

Joanne nodded, afraid to say anything because she wasn't quite sure of the control of her voice.

* * * * * * *

Ed Beckerman looked at Peter Scott, frowning, his lips tightly clamped together in thought.

"Pete," Ed said after a while, "I know this is throwing it at you fast, but I can't hold off business while you learn. What have you picked up about the Kelbore account?"

Peter Scott's face revealed nothing as he said:

"Well, first, its sales have been dropping during the last six months, since they went to the high quality slant in their advertising. Mr. Kelbore, Jr., a fifty-five year old southerner, is now in charge of the company—since the change of styling—and is in trouble, and I would guess, worried. He has strong religious beliefs, and from what I gather from his file, he's anti-sex, to a certain extent and—"

Beckerman laughed, said: "Stop right there."

"Why?" Peter asked, more puzzled sounding than worried.

"You were right about the religious part and the anti-sex...insofar as others are concerned. He doesn't like the idea of admitting the truth about life and himself—but throw a call girl in his direction and he jumps! He won't stand for anything sexy in his ads—but he's a real hard-core bastard!"

The disgust on the other man's face revealed his reaction to Ed's words. Peter's eyes narrowed and his lips became hard lines, his jaw set tight.

He said: "How the hell can people be like that?"

"Simple, my boy. He was raised to believe that sex was dirty—that you married a woman and she bore your children, but that sex, itself, was only for having children, and not for fun. He still believes that, but doesn't mind banging it with a whore—that lines up with his closed mind idea that sex is dirty. Now, tell me what else you know about Kelbore."

"Well, he seems to have a good product—I tried it last night, one shot," Peter said, grinning. "The only thing is, I'd say he would have a much better chance if he'd change his advertising style."

"Oh?" Beckerman inquired, surprised. He hadn't expected his new man to have any real ideas—not this soon in the game. And he wouldn't have expected Peter Scott to suggest them.

"Well, if he would start selling on a more human

level—with a good looking woman, and—"

"Oh, come on. You know right now that Hal Kelbore isn't about to do that. Anyway, thanks for the suggestion," Beckerman said a little heated. "But when we see Kelbore tomorrow, I would advise that you listen...just back me up."

Peter Scott nodded.

There was an awkward silence then, and Beckerman stood. "Here's the latest information on the account—our art department has done some pictures and layouts, and the copy department came up with some good ideas. Look them over and then try to remember every detail. Okay?"

"Fine," Peter said, standing and taking the large envelope that Beckerman handed him. As the young man stepped out of the office, Beckerman buzzed for his secretary.

Susan Sterling stepped into the room, closing the door behind her and sat in the chair in which Scott had been sitting.

She looked impersonally at Ed Beckerman and he felt a slow burning anger cut through him.

How lovely she looked, he thought irritated, wanting to take her in his arms.

She had on her yellow dress that showed off the well-shaped thrust of her breasts to an advantage that teased Ed with mental images of long nights of passion with her. She was calm, reserved, a shield was between her and him, invisible, but solid. No emotion showed in her gray-green eyes.

"Susan," Ed said, standing and stepping around the desk. "How long is this going to go on?"

She knew immediately what he meant, and the

sharp change in her eyes startled him. Instead of getting softer, the green seemed to ice over hard.

"Ed, I've been thinking about us. I...well, think maybe I should get another job."

The statement stunned Beckerman. He stood there unable to say anything for a moment. Finally the words came.

"Oh for God's sake, Susan. Don't give me that! I won't stand for it. I need you—desperately. You know how I feel about you and—"

"Yes," she said coldly, "I know *exactly* how you feel about me. And that's it, Ed. I don't want any more of it! It's finished. Complete. If you can just simmer down and listen to me calmly and—"

"Susan," he snapped, reaching for her, jerking her up to her feet. He pulled her against him. "I'm crazy about you! I—"

"I'm a plaything, Ed, and you know it. That's all it means to you—all it could mean to you—ever. I'm not that kind of girl. It was a mistake from the beginning. I don't want it." She was stiff and cold, like rock in his arms.

Slowly Ed released his secretary and stepped back, away from her.

"Can't you give it more serious thought?" he offered, shaken.

"I've given it thought." She shrugged and her eyes moistened. "Oh, Ed, you don't know what it's like. I...I...want you...more than you'll ever know. But not as the second woman—not on the back street—not in secret corners, hiding and afraid, ashamed. That's no way for a woman to live. It's not life! It never has been. I can't live that way. I don't want to. I...I didn't really know how...well, not until you just called me in...and I saw that light in your eyes—I wasn't sure. Now I am. I won't be a second woman in a man's life. And I won't ask you to divorce your wife, because I know you never would! The only thing I can do...is give you two weeks notice and—go look for another job."

Ed was thoughtful for a long time. Then he finally said: "We can't just cut it off like this. You have gone through this kind of thing before...and you've overcome it. It will pass. Think about it for awhile...before making that kind of plunge."

"It's settled, Ed. Sure it happened before. Sure I got over the depression. But each time it gets worse. It's no fun for you this way, and surely no fun for me. Stolen moments—that's not enough for any woman...in love!" With that she snapped around, and hurried out of the office.

Ed Beckerman stood there for a long time, shaking, sick inside.

//<u>Chapter Six</u>\\

Peter Scott had several double shots of whiskey—not Kelbore—at a bar, not far from where Paula Martin lived, before going up to her apartment. He was only slightly high from the effects of the liquor when he rang the doorbell.

Nervously he fingered the box of candy that he had bought for Paula, and waited for the door to open, feeling a hot sweat begin to form under his armpits.

The door opened and she stood there in a white, tight fitting, much too low cut dress that bound around her breasts as if straining to keep from spreading.

She looked like a she-goddess, standing there, smiling brightly, her hair done up on the back of her head, showing off the smoothness of her creamy neck and throat.

"Come on in," she invited, stepping back, her eyes flashing as he handed the candy over to her. "How nice." She closed the door and then moved across the room in a reserved swivel hipped motion.

"Make yourself at home," Paula said, putting the box of candy on a small table in the corner of the room. "I'll go get our drinks."

She briskly left the room, going into the kitchen.

Peter stepped over to a bookcase and began casually looking at the titles.

Paula walked into the room then, carrying a tray on which were two cocktail glasses and a cocktail shaker. She set the tray down on the glass-topped coffee table and settled onto the sofa. Her smile greeted him, warm, intrigued, amused.

Peter Scott stared at her for a long moment before moving toward the sofa.

She was all sex appeal. There was a wildly exciting thing about her whole body, the effect which she created. There were so many women who were sexy, but looked like something out of the whorehouse. Paula had that classic voluptuousness that a high-class call girl possessed, and then some. The extra plus factor was in her erotically shaped body, far more exciting than any call girl could have possessed and still made good in her profession. It was a combination of high charged sex appeal and class that was overwhelming to look upon.

"You know, Peter, I've been excited all day...I never have been so excited!" she told him, gleaming, reaching for the cocktail mixer.

"What's there to be so excited about?" he inquired, almost laughing to himself because he was almost on the verge of shaking from the powerful sight of her neckline.

"I don't know. Just that...well," she looked up into his eyes, pausing before filling the second cocktail glass, "I was anxious about, well, the two of us."

"Well, bottoms up!" Paula saluted, those laughing eyes twinkling playfully.

Peter laughed and finally felt completely relaxed as he took sip of the cocktail.

Later, while they were eating steaks, sipping chilled champagne, the liquor beginning to have its way on his brain, Peter began wondering just exactly what they were doing there. Exactly what was it that Paula Martin had in mind? She didn't seem the serious young thing, attempting to attract and impress a man into all her "wifely" charms. No, Paula was more like the jungle cat on the make.

As they finished off their dinner, Paula started to edge the conversation toward more intimate subjects. When she suddenly came out and asked: "Do you have some young thing on the string?" he stiffened, stared at her nervously.

"You shouldn't be worrying about such things," he offered, avoiding any answer to her question.

He sat there, smoking, listening to Paula move in the kitchen, trying to calm down the churning fires that were starting to burst their way up through him.

There was something very basic about the woman and about what she caused him to feel. Yet it was more than mere sexual craving to possess her; it was as if she held some kind of magic power that simply enveloped him with desire every time their eyes met. Or even when he merely looked at her. From the moment he had entered her domain he had felt an ever-growing magic and continual desire, that just kept wrapping itself tighter and tighter around his total being. Even when he tried to ignore it, focus on their conversation, that powerful erotic desire continued to ebb wildly in the background.

Paula came into the room, again swinging her hips in that wild way which kept his attention every time he watched her walking. She had a bottle of scotch whiskey in one hand and two glasses in the other.

Paula suddenly said: "Ed thinks the world of you, you know."

"No, I didn't," Peter admitted, surprised.

"You impressed him. I think you'll be around a long lime...and with a little help in the right places...if you know what I mean...it could be a fast climb upwards." She leaned closer, her red, lush lips only inches away from his. "You are a handsome animal."

At that moment time seemed to freeze, almost like a fantastically powerful picture had snapped into being in his mind. He saw her lips, her eyes, her body, the totality of her so painfully vivid that nothing else in the universe seemed to exist. There she was, merely inches away. This lovely Goddess, silently offering herself for the taking.

Suddenly, like lightening, like some devil had surged into him and taken control, like a wild man possessed, Peter moved. It was the action of a drunken man—both from booze and passions. The driving excitement of Paula's lush body, the nearness of her, and those full red lips just waiting to be kissed, drive him into action.

Peter crushed her to him, thrilled to the large softness of her giving breasts that cushioned themselves against his chest. Her mouth opened, wide, in quick offering. Her tongue darted out, savagely, greedily, hungrily, as if she couldn't stand waiting—like a woman who never waited to let things build up, but rather pushed them to the climax in a lustful need for the final actions of physical union.

Peter felt his head spinning from the effects of the liquor and the racy hotness of Paula's kiss.

She suddenly leaned backwards, her hand, on the back of his neck, tugging him down after her.

"My skirt," Paula moaned, releasing her grip on his shoulder, covering his ear with her lips, smothering herself against him as her hand reached down and fumbled with the zipper of her dress.

Peter helped her like a wild man, unable to think about anything other than the now complete insanity of his need, which she had created, and pushed up to the fullest power.

The magic of Paula simply enveloped him totally.

How their clothing disappeared, Peter didn't know. They went through a series of actions, which were both caresses and frantic attempts to undress. Then suddenly they were close, and then locked together.

He felt, heard, experienced the woman's deep need, her anguished cried, her thrusting wild movements which surged joyful pleasure over him. He was aware of hot sensation, needling sensation that flooded over him, moved like storm tossed waves, drowning all thought all immediate awareness of his surroundings. It was like being locked into some wild surreal dimension that jarred him out of the real world, away from the jungle civilization into which he had been born. This was a new kind of experience, a new kind of living, a thrill filled eternity which kept going and going through all the patterns of pleasure, all the teasing, wonderful pleasures that are normally saved for fiction writers, or erotic, make-believe dreams.

She tensed, she moaned, she ran wild, as if this moment meant as much to her as it meant to him. Only a moment, only an instant was he aware of the woman's reactions, only for a second of time did his attention center on the woman locked against him, then the visual world disappeared and was replaced by the fantasy which wrapped itself around him in a tight embrace, its hungry grip sending him upwards toward the peak of physical pleasure, slowly upwards to the crest of ecstasy and held him then, longer than he would have imagined possible.

Exhausted, sweating, his nerves and muscles on the verge of shaking, Peter moved away from the woman, away from the sofa, stood on weak legs. He looked down at Paula, amazed by what had just taken place, shocked dumb at how it had all happened.

Her eyes fluttered and opened. Cat green they looked up at him. "Oh, God, Peter," she managed between tortured lips. "Oh, God...Peter!"

Her arms reached up for him.

Peter took hold of her hands and she slowly moved, slowly came to a sitting position, and then stood, came into his arms, hugged herself close, trembling.

"Oh, Peter..." she moaned against his neck, clutching lighter.

They stood there for a long, long time, close, aware of the heat of one another, aware of the still surging passions which were under the surface of their exhaustion, just waiting to be released again.

How long they stood there, Peter didn't know. He was only aware of the strength reentering his body. He was only aware of the soft hotness of the woman's voluptuous body burning against his own, building the desire, despite his exhaustion.

Then, sometime, long, long after she had come into his arms, Paula made a subtle motion of her body, a subtle action that told all too clearly what she wanted.

They moved, stepped slowly toward the bedroom, where they would rediscover the ecstasy, the frantic wild perfection of their bodies joining in the ultimate union.

For a moment, just before they slipped down onto the bed, Peter thought about Joanne, and then shrugged off the thought. That was of the past; he was sure of that. Never in his life had he expected to meet somebody like Paula—never had he dreamed that there really existed such a female of lust. Now that he knew—it was impossible to even think about a Joanne Nestor.

//<u>Chapter Seven</u>\\

The next morning, when Peter drove to work, he turned his thoughts to the meeting that was supposed to take place that afternoon.

From what he knew about Kelbore, it was going to be an interesting meeting. It was also going to be interesting meeting the "big man" after having read and heard so much about him. Kelbore had arrived the evening before and Beckerman had gone out to meet him. Kelbore had a house in town, which was, from what Ed told Peter, a place where he had some pretty far out parties.

When Peter stepped into his office, Ann Fenneran looked up, smiled. "Mr. Beckerman wants to see you, right away!"

"Thanks."

A few minutes later Peter was in his boss' office.

Ed Beckerman said: "Are you on fire today?"

"About the Kelbore thing?"

"That's it!"

"Right."

Beckerman relaxed, said: "Any ideas?"

"Just what I told you...plus another addition. How about...well, Kelbore coming out with another line...one which will be sold a few pennies cheaper and sold with a sexy line...get at the more common public."

Beckerman shook his head. "Nothing doing! He wouldn't do such a thing!"

"Why not?"

"Because...you'll see. Kelbore is a hard man to do business with."

"Why not suggest it? It won't hurt."

Beckerman shook his head. "I wouldn't dare."

"What about me suggesting it?"

"We have a good layout and a good new direction. He'll bite on that."

Peter took a chance and said: "But that's merely a rewrite on the old approach. Culture, rich...crap!"

Beckerman's face drew serious. "So? It's something different. The wording is different and—"

"Okay...I'll listen."

Beckerman was silent for a while and then said: "Honestly, between you and me, I think the idea is good. But Kelbore could make things messy. I don't want the agency to look bad in his eyes. He spends thousands a week on advertising...and we get a good hunk of it. If you can impress him...you'll have the account in time. Do your best!"

Beckerman looked at his watch, said: "Well, he should be here in a few minutes."

It was well over ten minutes before the buzzer on Beckerman's desk sounded. He flicked a switch and a voice said: "Mr. Kelbore is here, sir."

"I'll be right out."

Beckerman rushed around his desk, went to the door, opened it and a moment later returned with a large, red-faced, fat man who turned steel gray eyes in

Peter's direction.

"This the young man you've been bending my ear about all last night?" Kelbore snapped in a clipped voice.

"Mr. Pete Scott. A good, bright young man." Kelbore extended his hand, and beefy fingers hugged against Peter's. "Glad to know you, son."

They settled into chairs and then Kelbore turned, asked Peter: "What do you think about the new spread?"

The question startled Peter. For a moment he didn't know what to say.

Beckerman came to his aid. "Pete's been working on another level of it, Ben."

"What end?"

"Research."

Peter quickly said: "I've seen a little of what's being done...but I wasn't in on the development."

"Oh?" Thick eyebrows arched into a question mark.

Beckerman said: "He just joined us a little while ago, and has been doing a lot of work in getting things organized. He'll be in charge of the account—on the production end, Ben."

"Oh?"

Kelbore had a way of saying "oh" that made it sound like a criticism. That, mixed with the hard, bland expression on his face gave the impression of a cruel, harsh man.

Defense cover-up? Peter wondered.

A little later his thoughts seemed to blur away. The throbbing suggestion of a hangover, which had kept with him since early that morning, was beginning to be a little stronger. He thought about Paula and the long night session they had shared. It had been revealing, exhausting and at the same time, invitingly exciting. It wasn't easy to make love to Paula and forget. His mind wandered, thinking about the lush excitement of the woman, the largeness of her wonderful breasts that had fairly quivered under his heated kisses.

All this time Beckerman was showing Kelbore the art layouts that had been made for the "new" approach.

Peter's eyes suddenly snapped to attention as he saw a slightly controlled suggestion of disapproval in the client's eyes. The reaction veiled over, fast.

Suddenly, Peter wondered if maybe his idea wasn't so bad after all. Maybe he should make the suggestion that was just bubbling over to be made. What did you have to lose?

Simply his job, maybe.

* * * * * *

Paula had never known such a wonderful feeling. It amazed her. She had never thought for a moment that Peter Scott would be any different from all the other men in her life.

Her whole body felt alive for the first time in years. She lay back in bed, dreaming about the long session the two of them had shared.

The bit on the couch had been overwhelming. It had been only the beginning. The session in the living room had merely offered a taste of what followed.

How wonderful. Wonderful man, wonderful lover, Peter Scott. The best there is, lady, the best there is!

The phone rang at that point.

She picked up the receiver.

It was her sister.

Diana Beckerman went through the first general actions of a polite social conversation, but right from the beginning Paula was aware that something was wrong.

When Diana asked what was new, Paula merely said that she'd been out with one hell of a man who had really swung.

"Who's the new lover?" Diana inquired in a strangely haunting voice t that was a mixture of vague interest and vague jealousy.

"Peter Scott. That's the guy Ed hired a little while ago...the other day, I think. Anyway—he's a real whacker!"

Diana laughed nervously and then after a long, awkward silence, Diana said: "Paula...I have to talk to you." She blurted out the last words as if afraid that if she didn't say them at that moment she would never say them.

For a moment Paula was too stunned to react verbally. She knew her sister well enough to realize exactly what kind of strain the woman was going through.

"What's wrong, honey?"

"Everything...just everything, Paula," Diana's voice came through the receiver almost tearfully. "I don't know where to turn—who to talk to. You're the only person in the world that I know who to talk to...who might be able to help me. Will you please, for God's sake, help me!" She screamed the last part in an almost hysterical voice.

Paula's heart jumped, frightened. "Oh, of course...

of course, anything Diana...anything in the world."

After a moment Diana said she'd be right over and then hung up.

Paula stood there, puzzled, worried, and almost frightened. What could it be? Diana wasn't the type of woman to get shook without good reason. All she could do was wait.

* * * * * * *

For Peter the meeting went well enough, considering that he wasn't called upon to make any important statements. That is, until towards the end.

But Peter couldn't help feeling a sense of depressing defeat as each minute went by.

Mr. Kelbore was a fat faced, hard man who looked at others as if they were the sin of the earth. He had that expression in his eyes that tried to accuse all others of the degenerate life he himself lived. The beat red of his face revealed the suggestion of a heavy boozer—which fitted to his profession as the owner and president of Kelbore Liquor.

Kelbore turned to Peter at one time during the session and said: "What would you like to suggest?"

Peter shook his head, smiling. "I don't think it would suit you, Mr. Kelbore."

Kelbore pushed his point. "Come on, boy. It can't be that bad."

"Well, I understand that it is a common practice to sometimes come out with another product—under another label, but with the same contents. It sells a little cheaper and—"

"I don't—"

"Please...I understand that. I'm not saying that you do this...I'm merely making a point," Peter announced, having decided to come on strong, to ignore the big man's bluff—which he had come to consider it. Kelbore made one face to the public and seemed to live another in private. Well, it was about time that somebody made him see the light.

Kelbore frowned for a moment, studied Peter and then strangely smiled. "Okay, young man—come on...give me hell!"

Ed Beckerman's jaw dropped an inch. His eyes widened.

Now Peter decided to dive in.

"Well, to be blunt. I know you don't like the idea of coming out with a second line—and that you don't like the idea of selling your whiskey on a more basic level and—"

"Basic level?" Kelbore asked, arching his eyebrows again.

"Basic is sexual level."

Ed Beckerman coughed nervously, said: "The boy doesn't understand that—"

"Please, Ed...no harm done. I like this new young man of yours. He has the guts to come out and speak. Go on!"

"Well, considering how you feel about this—I'd like to make a suggestion. I'd like to stick my head out and suggest that you come out with another line, with the same whiskey in it, and let me handle the selling—my way."

There was a long, long stony silence which followed that statement. The room seemed to get cold, icy cold, as if the North Pole had suddenly been thrust into the room.

Suddenly Kelbore stood, like he was shot from the chair.

Ed Beckerman quickly stood, said: "I hope you won't think that the agency has anything—"

Kelbore shook his head. His eyes centered on Peter's. "Come out to the house this evening. Mr. Beckerman knows the place. Bring a girl—if you have one who will come at the flick of a finger. I'll talk to you there."

With that, without saying anything more, Kelbore gripped hold of Peter's hand and then reached for Ed Beckerman. "You have a boy here. Keep hold of him."

Then, suddenly, the man turned, walked out of the office.

Beckerman stood there his jaw still open. Finally he said, "Well, I'll be damned and double damned."

As Peter walked out of the office and toward his own, he felt a sense of deflation shoot over him

Maybe he'd bitten off more than he could swallow.

//<u>Chapter Eight</u>\\

Paula fixed her sister some coffee, but put a good double shot of vodka into it. For herself she gulped down a couple of shots of scotch and then gave her own coffee a third shot. Then she returned to the living room, where Diana was sitting on the sofa, nervously smoking. Paula put the coffee on the glass-topped table in front of them.

"Well, sister mine, what do I owe this visit to?" Paula asked, trying to sound light and cheerful.

For a moment Diana hesitated and then reached for the coffee, took a sip, frowned, and quested her sister with her eyes.

"I thought you could use something."

"Vodka?"

Paula nodded.

Diana's green brown eyes studied Paula, who was dressed in a loose fitting off pink sweater—which didn't look so loose on Paula—and flaring dark gray skirt.

"You are an attractive witch!" Diana admired. "I never had the flare you had."

"Nuts and bolts! You never took the time."

"You're hair...it was always beautiful—mine..." Diana shrugged.

"You could fix that—and you know it."

"I just don't find the time," Diana said defensively.

Paula hesitated over her retort and then let it pass by. There was that in the tone of Diana's voice which was stiff, tight, and bitter. She decided to wait, listen and then see how things went. So far Diana hadn't said anything about what had brought her here.

"Paula, tell me about your new boyfriend."

Paula shrugged. "Just something special. Real special. I never knew a man quite like him. Oh, there've been others..." She considered seriously and then said: "Maybe I'm just getting to the point where the idea of settling down is a little more attractive."

What?" Diana exploded, surprised.

"Well, maybe I'm just talking." Paula took a strong swallow of the still hot coffee.

A long silence followed. Diana fidgeted nervously with her hands and then finally took a cigarette from the pack on the coffee table in front of her. Her hands were shaking as she lighted the cigarette. "I've got to stop smoking, one of these days."

"I've noticed...you never were much of a smoker—just until lately," Paula said, taking the lead and quickly adding: "What's the trouble?"

They were silent for a long time, then Diana started asking Paula about Peter Scott. It was an attempt to keep the conversation going, away from the topic that had brought her there. Paula played along. They talked for a long time, and the conversation drifted from Peter to other men, then to their childhood and a little later to the first men they'd had.

That's when Diana came, suddenly, directly to the point.

"Paula, you've always been good with men! I've failed. Like mother."

There was such bitterness in Diana's voice that Paula knew immediately that the moment of serious conversation had finally arrived.

She sat there for an awkward moment, not quite sure what to say. Then she decided that it would be best to be blunt. The first tall drink had already almost disappeared from Diana's glass, and the woman was already beginning to show signs of drunkenness.

"What do you mean, Diana?"

Hesitance, then: "I just don't...like it!"

"Sex?"

"Sex!"

"You never had a man...before Ed, did you?" Paula inquired.

For a moment Diana didn't do anything, then she lowered her eyes, nodded her head. "He was the first..."

"And only man?"

"Yes," she said in a small voice.

"Then...maybe that's the trouble," Paula suggested.

"But that doesn't help."

"Why not?"

"Oh...you should know. I'm married and can't..."

The silence after that was long. Diana finished off her drink, then indicated she wanted more. Paula gave her a stiff second.

Diana said: "I'm...afraid...I'm losing Ed."

Silence, long and awkward, then: "I don't know what to do...I'm scared...scared to death, Paula."

"Can I be personal?"

"God, please."

"How is it with you and Ed. Does he...make love to you?"

"Yes...once a week...after he's drunk enough. Then...then it's...nothing!" Tears streamed do Diana's cheeks. "What can I do?"

"What do you do...well, when Ed makes love to you?" Paula asked, feeling an icy chill race through her. It was hard as hell to come right out and say it, but there was no other way. "You just lay there and...wait for him to—"

"Oh, Paula, I know that's all wrong. I...I tried...but...I don't know...it's as if I can't wait for him to get through...I can't...he sometimes almost makes it and...but...it never...I know it's all my fault. There's something wrong with me...I know that—but isn't there something that I can do...some way that I can keep Ed? I know that I won't the way things are going. It's been getting worse and worse...it's only a matter of time!"

"I'm no authority...I can't tell you what to do, Diana," Paula warned her.

"Please...you...you are so...well, you know how to please a man and—"

"Diana...believe me...the problem isn't how to please a man—it's how a man can please you! I don't think there's anything wrong with you that a good old-fashioned intelligent sex party wouldn't cure. And not with your husband. The first thing you have to do is convince yourself that there's nothing wrong with you—after that...well, believe me, everything will come quite naturally—you'll know exactly what to do—and you will want to do anything—and I mean anything to Ed—keep a man happy in bed and you have him...where it hurts the most!" Paula had spit out the last words as if they were hot bullets.

Diana sat there saying nothing, the expression on her face was that of a woman who has been slapped, hard, but knows she deserves it.

She sighed, a deep, racking, painful sigh. "I couldn't."

"You have to."

After a long time Diana asked: "But...I'm married and wouldn't know how...how could I? I...how could I do such a thing?"

"There are a lot of ways. You have to find your own. But believe me, it's quite easy to seduce a man—very, very easy. Just let him know what you want, act sexy as hell, and make it impossible for him to turn you down. He'll get the message where it will do him the most damage—after that...let nature take its course."

"But..."

"But nothing! Either that...or go to some doctor and see if he can help you!" Paula said forcefully. "Either you're serious about this or you're just fooling yourself. Why haven't you talked to Ed about it?"

"I couldn't."

"Well, that's your problem. But believe me, it can be a lot of fun, if you know what to do—how to enjoy it. I was lucky—I guess. I learned fast, found out that I liked it...I didn't worry about the rights and wrongs...maybe my life's been a little faster than some, but I've never tried to hurt anybody. Bedtime with me has been fun and games with no strings attached. I demand nothing—I try to have a ball—and it's been fun. The single girl has a right to have her fun, too. But the wife has a right, too. And if she doesn't get it at home...and is afraid of being frigid, she should go to a doctor—and if that doesn't help— hell, she should do what is necessary to find out the truth about herself.

"Diana, please believe me, until you discover for yourself that sex can be enjoyable with a man...well, you won't enjoy it. Not until you understand that there's nothing wrong with you will you find emotional relief. If necessary, go out and get some guy— go to a motel with him...hell, I could arrange something for you, private, some weekend...we could go in the mountains, together, for a little trip. Then you could find out exactly how you feel."

Paula reached for her sister's hand "Why don't we do that?"

"I don't know...I couldn't do it that way..." Diana said, weakening.

"Okay, do it your own way. But find some way to prove to yourself that you can enjoy it. Talk to Ed, if you have to, if you can't do that go to a doctor...do something! Why don't you try making the advances toward Ed one night...take the lead and keep it. And you can keep it, if you want to."

"What good will that do? I want to...I want the man to make me want him...not me make him want me. Hell, Ed would just lay back and enjoy it!" Diana cried. "And I can't cheat on him!"

Paula considered that, then decided to say:

"How do you know he hasn't cheated on you?"

Diana's face snapped back in alarm. Her eyes widened, her features drew tight, became white.

"I...I...God...hope he hasn't!" But there was doubt

in her eyes, as if she really knew the truth.

Paula couldn't help thinking that Diana did know the truth about her husband and that was the real reason for her being here.

"Consider the possibility! If he is…you can't blame him…considering how you are so totally disinterested in sex. Men want their women to enjoy sex…how do you think he feels, knowing you don't enjoy it? A terrible ego-crunch for him. So…why shouldn't a man get his ego recharged with somebody who can do just that. There are plenty of women out there in the world willing to offer themselves up to any man, married or not! No strings attached." She laughed almost nervously, then added: "Look at me! I'm one of them!"

Diana was quite for a long moment, her eyes finally met Paula's, searchingly.

"You have options, make use of them is my best advice!"

"Maybe you're right," Diana breathed out. "Maybe, damn it all, you're right!"

After that it was only a matter of a short time before Diana made a fumbling excuse to leave.

As Paula watched her sister through the front room window, climbing into the large convertible which her husband had bought her some time ago, she felt a pang of guilt and a pang of sadness.

Maybe it had been a mistake. But on the other band, she had given the only advice she knew how to give; the only honest advice she could possibly give her one and only sister.

//<u>Chapter Nine</u>\\

In his office, Peter considered the invitation Kelbore had made to him to come over to the man's town house for the evening. It was obvious what kind of evening the man had m mind, and it was just as obvious that somebody like Joanne Nestor wouldn't be the type of woman to bring along.

He buzzed his secretary, said to get Miss Martin on the line.

A little later he was talking to Paula. "...and that's the way it stands," he said, after having told her about the conference. "I was wondering if you could make it for the evening?"

She jumped at the chance.

A little later, after having finished his phone conversation with Paula, Peter called Ann Fenneran into the office.

"Relax," Peter told his secretary. "I just wanted to talk. I don't think there's anything too pressing...is there?"

"Just the files and—"

"But they could be done later?"

She nodded.

"Had a lunch break?" Peter asked.

She hesitated as uncertain. Then she said: "Not

yet."

He considered the realities. She was an attractive woman. He couldn't help wondering if she would allow a relationship to develop between herself and a man she worked for. An interesting thought.

Then he felt a stab of guilt. First Paula, now Ann? What about Jo?

Peter suddenly realized something that had avoided him for the last twenty-four hours. Joanne was of the past. Finished. Just like that. As if he'd been riding on one train for a long time, but once off, never wanted to get on again. He felt a sense of guilt at first, then a sense of relief.

Maybe it had been nothing more than a joyride— merely fooling himself. Joanne had been part of his childhood and his young manhood—and part of the life he'd led with his parents.

"Ann," he said, "how about lunch?"

The way she jumped at the offer was almost too revealing. "I'd love to!"

* * * * * * *

Kelbore had a large, two-story house that was set back away from the street, in front of a long, large green lawn. As Peter pulled his car to a stop in front of the house, he took a deep breath, turned off the engine and turned to face Paula.

She was dressed in deep green, which set off the color of her eyes, and the red flame of her long hair. She smiled, reached over and patted Peter's cheek.

"What's there to worry about?" Paula inquired.

"Who's worried?"

As they came onto the porch, the door suddenly opened and a youngish man stood there looking out at Peter.

"Well, hello, Paula," the man said.

Paula tensed against Peter. "This is Kelbore's son, Tom," she said in a subtly stiff voice.

"Tom...Peter Scott," Paula introduced, as they stepped into the large hallway.

The two men shook hands and then the front door was closed like the clanging of a jail cell.

"Well, Dad told me a lot about you, Pete," Tom Kelbore said, leading the way down the hall toward a room from which music was coming. "We plan on a nice little party. There're a couple of girls here for Dad and me and well, I know how Paula is..." He grinned and reached over and patted Paula's arm.

The intimacy of the action annoyed Peter. He didn't like the idea of another man being on more than mere friendly terms with Paula. But he told himself that he was coming in on Paula, no doubt, after a long list of past lovers. If Tom was one of them well, he'd just have to get used to it.

They were ushered into a large room that was furnished in heavy, expensive pieces Music seemed to be coming out of the walls, on each side of a large brick fireplace

Two quite attractive women were sitting near a large home bar in the corner of the room. Each had enough breast exposure showing to fill more than two dresses. There was something about them that immediately seemed to scream professional. What made him think that, Peter couldn't be sure. Possibly because of what he'd heard about Ben Kelbore.

"Jenny and Nickie, Paula and Peter," Tom introduced quickly with a wave of his hand.

Jenny was tall, dark haired and cool. Nickie was the heavier of the two—which meant that her breasts were far larger. They were both strikingly attractive women.

Paula hardly nodded.

"Drinks?" Tom offered.

"Scotch," Peter suggested.

Drinks were handed around and then Tom, said: "If you want, Paula, you can show him around a bit. I have to see Dad about something...the girls can entertain themselves."

"Fine," Paula said in an almost relieved voice, hugging Peter's arm tighter.

"Sorry, Pete, but Dad was tied up late... just got home a little while back—had to change. I was looking for you...explains the quick greeting!" The man grinned and left.

Paula quickly took Peter out of the room, and said: "Those girls...they're for pay!"

"I gathered...what about this Tom, Paula?"

"He's a wild cat...tomcat," she laughed. The drinks they'd had a little while before coming to the Kelbore house were beginning to get to her. "Like father, like son!"

"But...isn't that slightly awkward? I thought Kelbore...well, was sort of a religious man, rather tight-lipped and such and..."

"And he is. But son Tom is a swing cat, too. From what I learned...well, Tom started early. He discovered his father with strange girls and well that was the beginning."

"What's in line for the...well, evening?"

"How would I know?" Paula offered, smirking.

"How come you know so much about the business...being that you don't work for the company?" But Peter had already guessed the answer to that one.

"I knew Tom," Paula admitted in a small voice. She took him through the lower half of the house, which was made up of half a dozen rooms. Living, play room, bedrooms, study, dining room, and kitchen. All were furnished like Kelbore had so much money he didn't know what to do with it all.

"Quite a place," Peter observed as they started back to the living room.

When they returned to the living room, Ben Kelbore was there, a tall drink in his hand, his eyes glassy. He jerked across the room to them, grinning.

"Paula," he beamed, leaning close and kissing her lips.

"Peter," he greeted, pumping his hand.

After a moment he said: "Well, let's get on with it."

He motioned them to a low couch which was a little to the right of the one on which the two women and Tom were sitting. "We have a real fun time coming on. I'll flick the switch, and everything will roll!"

As they settled themselves, the lights suddenly dimmed and Paula leaned closer to Peter, her large breast pressing into his arm. She squeezed his hand and then placed it down to her thigh.

There was a sound of movement behind them and Peter turned to see part of the wall open up. Then as he returned his attention to what was going on in front of them, he saw a screen drop from the ceiling.

A warning grind hit the pit of his stomach. What kind of films could they be showing? Certainly nothing about Kelbore. Whiskey, and not some film that could be seen in any movie house.

It was obvious from what he'd learned about Ben Kelbore.

Light flickered on the screen and then a scene sprayed on.

A woman, naked, stretched out on a bed, looked directly at him. She said in a low, deep voice: "I'm Karen...and what you are about to see is something very special. I believe it's about time that people learned something about sex...I mean, real sex! Learn something they couldn't learn from their wives!"

She laughed throatily and then cupped hands under her large naked breasts.

Then two men stepped to her side as she stretched out full length on the bed.

They went through motions, through passages of physical exercise, which were unnerving to watch. There was nothing sexy, in his mind, to what was happening on the screen. All he could think of was that sometime it had to end. When the screen went black, Kelbore stood, flicked a light, turned to the two women on the sofa with him and his son, said: "Why don't you girls give us a real party show? Something that'll really get things going."

Paula squirmed against Peter, and he felt the somewhat uncomfortable. This time it was a personal thing.

How could a woman like Paula stand such a set up? What kind of woman was she, really? He'd learned to accept her sexual brazenness and excitement, but this was something cheap and dirty.

The expression in her green eyes, as they met his, revealed that she'd read his disgust. She leaned closer, whispered softly in his ear; "We're here, there's nothing we can do but make the most of it."

Paula stood quickly, took hold of Peter's hand. "Come...I'll show you where to have a real live ball."

Without a word, Peter followed Paula and was aware of the other two couples getting up and following them out of the room.

Paula walked down the hallway and then came to one of the bedrooms in which they had looked some time before. She opened the door and then closed it behind them when they had walked into the room.

"You didn't like it, did you?" she asked, opening her purse and taking out a pack of cigarettes. Peter was shaking, his body covered with sweat. Finally he managed to shake his bead from side to side.

Paula lighted a cigarette and then took it out of her mouth, putting it into his. "There, you'll feel better...after a while," she said casually. Lighting another Kent, she moved to the large double bed, unzipped her dress, which she allowed to fall to the floor. She sat, looked across at him, studying Peter in a serious manner. "You don't have to take this kind of thing, Peter. I could talk to Ed."

Peter was about to say something, and then she quickly saved him from doing so.

"Why don't you come over here?" Paula suggested.

Like a zombie possessed, Peter stepped forward, and by the time he was in front of Paula, she had unlatched her bra and let it slip off her large, hefty breasts.

The sight of that large supple flesh, dotted by the bright pink of her nipples, excited a burn through Peter. For a moment he tried to hold it off, he attempted to stop it; he thought, what the hell!

Either here, or in his or her apartment—or a motel or hotel. What difference did it make?

He leaned down and she slowly stretched out on the bed. His lips covered one breast.

After that he wasn't thinking about anything but the softness and the warmth of the woman on the bed with him.

Later, much later, lying in the darkness, after having turned out the light, Peter thought about Joanne Nestor, but there was no sense of guilt this time, and he thought about Ann Fenneran. And it was the image of Ann Fenneran which held his attention for a long, long time, until Paula's hand caressed his thoughts back to her, until her hungry lips covered his, her tongue surged deep into his mouth.

Then he was only thinking about the female devil who was in complete possession of his physical needs she so furiously fired.

//<u>Chapter Ten</u>\\

Ed Beckerman sat by the fireplace, warning himself. He was thinking about the Kelbore "party," which he knew was going on. Purposely Kelbore hadn't invited him. It was one of those arrangements between them. When a new man was found to handle Kelbore's account, it was set up so that Kelbore could feel the guy out, see how they might work together—on what level their relationship might be handled.

Ed's wife, Diana, was sitting, reading, and then after a while she put down the book, looked up at her husband and said: "You know, Paula seems to have taken a liking to your new guy."

Ed's mind snapped out of his mental wanderings and his eyes jerked to his wife. "What's that about Paula?"

"She's seeing this...what's his name? Some guy you just hired. Something Scott...I remembered the last name because of the Scott Paper Company," she said with a laugh.

Ed frowned. "Peter Scott?"

"That's it."

"What's going on between the two of them?" Ed asked, annoyed.

"I think something serious, this time."

86

It was the way in which Diana made that statement which caught and held Ed Beckerman's attention.

"Paula, serious?" he cried, surprised.

"I really believe so."

Ed thought about that. The little tramp, the slut who spread her goodies for every guy who was willing to give her a good evening on the town, getting serious. It didn't seem possible

It was sometime later, when he was in bed, that Ed's mind began to form a plan. At first he revolted from it, and then the more he thought about it, the more intriguing it became. Like a man who is addicted to dope and sees a package of "stuff" on the table before him, Ed saw his way into the bedroom with Paula. The way might be filled with dirt, but it was a way.

* * * * * * *

Joanne Nestor had been in a terrible anguish ever since seeing Peter that last time.

She couldn't help thinking that no matter how things had been that night, their relationship was crumbling, and desperately, like a drowning person in the middle of the ocean, she was frantically attempting to find some way to survive, some way to keep hold of what little happiness she now possessed.

One time, long before, Peter had suggested that they move into an apartment together. That was before he'd finally decided to get a job of his own, away from his father's furniture store. Joanne had been embarrassed and shocked and let him know exactly how she'd felt.

Now she wondered if it hadn't been a terrible mistake.

She slipped out of bed, picked up the phone, dialed work, got her boss on the phone, and said she was sick and couldn't make it that day.

Then she picked out her most attractive dress, a black cocktail dress which revealed a healthy supply of her breasts, and hugged every curve of her bouncy figure. She took her time dressing and then ate a quick breakfast of coffee and one fried egg. Afterwards she went out to her car and headed for the offices of Lancer Advertising Inc, in the center of town.

* * * * * * *

For Peter the night had been depressing to the point where he'd gotten drunker than he had wanted to. The next morning was hangover time. When he looked at himself in the mirror, he saw a haggard face, blood shot eyes, sagging lips.

"You've had it, buddy!" he groaned.

Before last night, Peter had believed there was another side of Paula. But seeing her at the party, obviously enjoying herself, knowing what was going to happen, and not being upset, but actually seemingly to look forward to it, had turned the emotional tide away from her.

And what was left?

Joanne was the first thought.

But that was already of the past. He didn't want to turn back, to seek out what had once been his life.

//<u>Chapter Eleven</u>\\

Peter Scott was sitting in his office, trying to think of some way to approach Ann Fenneran, when the buzzer sounded.

"Yes?" he said, leaning across the large desk. "A Miss Joanne Nestor is here to see you,"

Ann's voice sounded over the intercom.

For a startled moment Peter felt a flush of embarrassment, as if Joanne had been reading his mind.

"Have her come in," he said a moment later. Joanne looked beautiful, he thought, startled by the sight of her. It seemed ages, rather than just a day or so, since he'd seen her.

"Well, how's my lover?" she inquired, meeting his eyes with a level gaze.

"I'm fine, Jo, and you?" he asked formally.

She flinched as if slapped. Then, taking a deep drag said: "I was wondering what you were doing for lunch."

The statement was made in a voice which revealed to Peter that she was desperately unsure of herself. After having known each other for so long, it was possible to feel, to even personally experience the mood that the other was in.

"Jo," he finally said, "maybe we should have lunch

together—talk things out."

"That sounds...really...serious," she countered, shifting in her seat. After a long moment of silence, she leaned forward, her blue eyes glistening, serious, probing his. "What's happening to us?"

"To us?" he asked, as if puzzled by the question. What a coward he was. Why didn't he just come out and say it was finished, that it wasn't anybody's fault, that he really didn't feel any different towards her than he'd ever felt—but rather that he had learned what the emotion had been—how shallow it had been.

"It's finished, isn't it?" Joanne suddenly blurted out, tears running down her cheeks

"Jo...please...take it easy and—"

"Take it easy?" she fairly screamed at him. After all we've...Peter, the least you can do is tell me the truth. Just where do we stand?" Emotion choked in his own throat. He wanted to rush around the desk, pull her into his arms, and say that it wasn't her fault, that things had happened to make him see himself for what he was, to see his future life, as he wanted it to be.

"Jo, believe me...I didn't want it to...be like this and—"

"And it *is* finished!" she rasped out softly, defeated.

"I'm trying to find myself," Peter said quickly, hoping it wouldn't be necessary to come right out and tell her the truth.

Joanne stood suddenly, glaring at him. "Why don't you have the guts to tell me the truth?"

Silence was the only answer he could give her. "Either or, Peter. How is it? Do I get my freedom—or is it marriage?"

It was the desperate last stand of a woman who is drowning and knows there's no straw to grab for, but is still trying.

"It's...finished!" Peter choked out, his eyes closing against that pain which rushed up through him

Just like that. It was finished, sealed...completely—the end. New book, new woman, new life. Future. Where?

Then he was aware of a voice.

"Peter Scott!" Ann Fenneran's voice snapped out of the surrounding blur that had been his awareness for too many long, frantic minutes.

Peter opened his eyes and looked at the attractive secretary who was standing in front of his desk, her face frowning, worried.

"What did you do to that girl?" Ann inquired in a harsh tone of voice. But there was something in the woman's eyes that told him she had guessed most of what had happened.

"We were engaged. Unofficially, sorta. It's part of the past, now," he managed.

There was an awkwardness between them for some moments. Then Ann sighed, said: "I'm sorry, Peter."

"Don't be. It's better this way," Peter told her, trying to smile, but not quite making it. Then he asked: "How about dinner tonight?"

Ann Fenneran blinked at him, her mouth opened as if to say something and then slammed shut. She studied him, her mouth pursing in thought, then finally said: "Why not?"

* * * * * * *

Ed Beckerman had brooded in his office, going through the actions of work, for some hours before he got the courage to go through with the plan he had worked out in his mind the night before. He picked up the phone, on his desk, dialed for an outside line, and then dialed Paula's number.

It was some moments before the ringing came to a stop and a sleepy voice said: "Hello?"

"Paula?"

"Yes."

"Ed, Paula."

"Oh, what the hell do you want this time of the morning?"

"It's past eleven, Paula," he scolded in a friendly voice. "I wanted to see you."

"What about?"

"Something personal. It's important. How about lunch?"

"Where...I'll hardly have time to dress and—"

"At your place?" Ed offered boldly.

Paula finally said: "Okay. I'll throw something on."

"Fine, I'll be over at one thirty—that should give you time to get lovely."

As Ed Beckerman hung up the phone, he felt a nervous sense of satisfaction. Then he buzzed his secretary and said that he would be out for the rest of the afternoon and to cancel all calls.

* * * * * * *

Paula dressed, hurriedly made up her face and then

went into the kitchen to start to fix lunch. All the time her mind was whirling over the phone call from Ed Beckerman. At first she'd thought it was something about her sister, but that last remark had sent a horrified chill through her body.

Paula attempted to brush aside such thoughts, and turned her thinking to Peter Scott.

He had been wonderful the other night. The way his body had united with hers, the way he had given such thrills to every nerve in her, had overpowered Paula. What she had believed to be true before, was now a proven fact as far as she was concerned. She was falling in love for the first time.

When the doorbell rang, Paula was just finished with making the coffee. She hurried into the front room and a moment later let Ed Beckerman into the living room.

Ed looked at her, at the apron that draped over the front thrust of her breasts. The expression in his eyes suddenly alarmed Paula and reminded her of his last flippant remark.

"You look lovely, Paula," he said, leaning closer to her, as she quickly closed the door.

Paula skillfully slipped away from any closeness with Ed and glided across the room toward the kitchen. "I'll be ready in a moment."

"Have something to drink?"

She returned to the living room a few moments later with two glasses of whiskey on the rocks. The stiff drink she'd downed just before filling her glass, was bubbling in her stomach.

Paula took a sip from the glass and was about to return to the kitchen, when Ed quickly said, reaching for her wrist and pulling her down to him on the sofa. "Relax, I want to talk to you. Lunch can wait."

Paula plunked down onto the sofa, startled. "What is it?"

For a moment the man hesitated and then he squared his shoulders, said: "I don't want you seeing Peter Scott again."

Stony silence slammed down between them. Then Paula said: "What the hell?"

She glared at her brother-in-law, not able to quite believe her ears.

"I mean it, Paula," Ed said rather forcefully—too forcefully. There was a strange gleam in his eyes that warned her.

"Why?" she snapped. "What business is it of yours?"

"He's working for the firm—do you think it is a good idea for one of the executive's relatives going out with a newly hired hand?" Ed pointed nastily out.

"Oh, come on—since when did it matter who I went out with?" Paula felt that sick sensation rush over her.

"Oh, but it does." Ed stared evenly at Paula and then asked: "What difference does it make to you, Paula?"

"A lot," she snapped back angrily.

"A lot...how much?" There was a thin smile beginning to choke the corners of his mouth. As he sat there, staring at her, his eyes narrowed just slightly, his face leaned a little closer, looked like some watchful watchdog.

"Hey, what is this, Ed? Since when have you become so interested in my personal life? You've never tried to interfere before!" She started to stand and felt herself yanked back down next to the man. Ed's right hand hurt her arm where his fingers squeezed.

The cold gleam in the man's eyes seemed to turn to steel. "I've been interested for a long time, Paula, and you know it. Now I think we can change things around a little." His breathing was hard in her ears, his eyes now suddenly bright and full. "I've wanted you, Paula—and now I think you'll see things my way!"

Paula's eyes widened and a low anguished sound broke from her lips. She could hardly believe what was happening.

"You must be kidding, Ed," was all she could think of to say.

"Diana tells me you are really hooked on him…well, I'll just see how hooked you are. You play around right with me, Paula and I won't fire Peter. I'll let him keep his job, just as long as you play things my way." His voice was hard now, and Paula realized that he must have had something strong to drink before arriving. The man wasn't really making any sense. What the hell caused him to believe it was possible to blackmail her into an affair with her sister's husband? She attempted to stand, but couldn't. The man's strong hand held her down on the sofa. "Ed! What the hell's gotten into you?"

"Nothing!" he told her. "Just that I've wanted that body of yours for a long time. You've pushed it around my face just too long. I can't stand it without having you, I can't stand it knowing that you spread for anything with pants on. And there's nothing wrong with me! There's no reason why we can't have a wild time of it! And you know that. So…I just thought I'd make you realize how I felt." He suddenly stopped talking and his lips grinned wide.

What a real bastard the man was!

What was happening was just too fantastic! Disgusted, Paula jerked away from her brother-in-law, stood over him, the glass of whiskey clutched tightly in her hand. She thought about her sister, and what Diana had told her the day before, and felt the sickness eat its way up through her. How could a guy be like this?

Suddenly the glass and hand moved and the whiskey slashed out across Ed Beckerman's face.

"That's your answer!" Paula cried, thrilling to what she'd just done.

Ed moved much faster than she would have thought possible. The man leaped to his feet, his hands shot outwards, yanked at Paula's shoulders, slammed her body against his own. His lips covered over hers, brutally.

It was like trying to fight with an enraged bear. There just wasn't any arguing. She relaxed in the man's grip, remaining unresponsive, waiting for him to finish with his little show.

"Ed!" Paula yelled at him, terror gripping her throat and chest. "What are you—?"

"Just be quiet, Paula, you'll like this!" He slammed the door of her bedroom and shoved her onto the bed. Glaring down, Ed said: "Now it's about time we understood each other. I want you Paula. I'm going to have you, one way or another. I've made up my mind about that I can't continue without having you. I've thought about you ever since the other night. It's driving me out of my mind—and now I have the lever to

96

get what I want. Either you make up your mind that there's no difference between me and other men—or I see to it that your man Peter Scott is fired, as of now!"

Paula sighed and then a thrill waved through her as she realized there actually was no escape. Peter would be fired. And if she didn't give into Ed now, the man would only wait until he had really found a way to get what he wanted.

The thrill hardened to sudden desire, as if now that she had a rationalization to lean upon, the idea of seducing Ed excited and intrigued her

How many times had she wondered what it would be like with Ed Beckerman? How many times had she had to fight down a natural and instinctive animal desire for the man, just because he was her sister's husband.

And really, whose fault was this? If Diana had kept her man happy at home, she'd have never had to worry about Ed leaping into another woman's bed. It was Diana's problem and—fault.

She sighed again and then the wave thrilled up through her stronger this time.

"Okay, Ed, anything you say," she finally told the man, standing.

"That's better," he grinned, moving toward her. "That's much better. I'm glad you saw the light."

As Paula let the man fold her into his arms, she kept telling herself that this was for Peter Scott, was for the man she now fully believed herself to be in love with.

This is Diana's fault, not mine! she told herself. And then she became the she-cat, the devil of feminine love, the passionate animal that could only respond to a man's sensual kisses, his voluptuous kisses, and his hot caresses.

The clothing slipped from their bodies. They moved to the bed. And they embraced.

In the next moments the only things Paula was thinking about were the sensations that jerked over her body, tightened her muscles, and, in the end, burned her brain in searing hot ecstasy.

//<u>Chapter Twelve</u>\\

As Peter danced with Ann Fenneran, he felt a strange elation that hadn't really reached into his life for some time. The long affair with Joanne, which had finally ended that afternoon, and his own struggle with himself for so long, combined with the sex parties with Paula Martin, had left an aftermath of depression. Being with Ann was rather nice, a lovely kind of escape from everything that had taken place before; she was a totally new experience.

They had gone to dinner, after he'd picked Ann up at her apartment, and now they were at the Copa Club, one of the few places in the city where a couple could have an intimate, romantic evening on the town.

They danced for a long time, the rhythm of the music winding itself through their bodies, gently pressing them against one another in a lightly intimate fashion that created mental promise for what might, in time, develop between the two of them.

When the music stopped and the combo took off for a break, they returned to the small table, where their half finished drinks still were sitting, waiting for them. They settled down into their seats and Ann's thigh accidentally touched his. It was a pleasant touch, sending a wave of desire through him.

"Ann, you are a beautiful woman," he told her, taking hold of one of her delicate hands, folding his fingers around hers.

"Why, Peter, how nice," she grinned. The drinks they had consumed had obviously gotten to her. She pressed her thigh against his again.

"What's a nice girl like you working her head off at a firm like Lancer?" Peter wanted to know a moment later, after lighting cigarettes for both of them.

"I have to make a living," she pointed out. "Nobody is supporting me, yet."

"Sounds promising."

"It's always promising."

"Can I ask you a personal question?"

She stared at him for a moment and then smiled. "That depends."

"Why haven't you gotten married?"

"The right man never came around," she admitted.

"Surely you've had offers."

"Offers—but a girl doesn't have to take them up, does she?" she countered, her eyes twinkling. "How about you?"

"Nix. I almost made it, with Joanne."

"What about her, Peter?" Ann asked seriously.

"Well, it's a long story, Ann. I knew Jo most of my life. We almost grew up together—but never really started going out, romantically, until a few years back. Things got seriously involved and I guess we were in love—in a way. But there are all sorts of love. I never really understood that until just a little while ago. Jo wanted to get married...well, it never came about. I guess I understand why, now."

"There's nothing wrong with that, Peter."

100

"Hell, of course there is!" He knew that the drinks had gotten to him, too. "Jo wanted home and family—now. She didn't want to wait. She pushed. I just wasn't ready. But now that I think of it, I don't think it was because of the job...it was because I wasn't sure of how I felt about Jo."

"Is any man sure of how he feels about the woman he loves—until the moment of truth?"

"Of course!"

"You really believe that?"

"I know it. The moment came today...and I'll admit I was depressed. But I guess that's natural."

In the semi-darkness of the small nightclub, Peter was sure that Ann's cheeks flushed at that moment.

She is lovely, he thought. *So damned lovely. More lovely than I realized!*

It was some time later that they suddenly decided to leave. It was well past twelve by the time they got into his car and started towards her apartment. No words were exchanged about where they would be an hour later, but it wasn't really necessary.

Peter couldn't help thinking about what it would be like to make love to Ann, to hold her body gently to his, to kiss her lips, to caress her breasts, to explore all the secrets of her body. It was a wonderful and pleasant dream that he was determined to make come true.

As they parked in front of her apartment, Ann opened her purse, pulled out a pack of cigarettes.

They sat there smoking for several seconds without saying anything. It was Ann who broke the silence.

"Peter...you're a nice guy. I've really enjoyed myself this evening." She turned looked up into his eyes. She was still sitting on the far side of the car, but there was an intimacy in her eyes that seemed to almost embrace him. He could easy read the desire that welled there, silently, longingly.

He reached for her and folded his arms around her. Drawing Ann close, he murmured, "It's been wonderful...really wonderful."

"Yes," she breathed, looking up into his eyes like a lost little girl. "Wonderful."

Then they kissed again. But this time it was passionate, hot and fiery. The pressure of her dear form against his made him feel as if he'd been plugged into some wall socket charged with sexual electricity. It was fantastically numbing.

Her tongue darted deep into his mouth as she strained against him. Then just as quickly as it had begun, it stopped.

"I better go in," she said, hurriedly pulling away from him.

"Alone?"

"I think it best!" But her smile revealed the hot desire ebbing through her whole body.

A moment later she was in the apartment.

* * * * * * *

As Ann slipped into bed, she found it impossible to keep her mind away from thoughts intimately between herself and Peter.

It was a funny thing about men who hadn't learned the by-ways to women's bedchambers. They believed that a woman was something that had to be protected, kept safe from being seduced.

Yes, Ann told herself, she would have to plan very,

102

very carefully if she wanted to marry this man. And, strangely enough that idea was far from unappealing. That, in part, was why she had not let things go beyond that wildly hot kiss. She knew it would be so very easy to fall in love with Peter. And any intimacy happening between them had best be in such a manner that it wasn't cheapened—if she wanted something serious.

Fall in love? she questioned herself. *How could that be?* They didn't even know one another. Yet, love was a strange emotion; and it didn't always follow simple logic.

Hell, she was already falling, and good!

* * * * * * *

When Ed Beckerman had left her, Paula lay on the bed for a long time, deep in terrible guilt, sick inside about what had happened. In the race of passionate need, physical hunger that had burst so alive in her, she'd been unable to feel anything other than that need.

Tears welled in her eyes and then streamed down the side of her face. Finally Paula sat up and went into the kitchen, got a bottle of whiskey and tipped it over her lips.

How did things get into such a mess, so suddenly?

But, of course, she realized, it hadn't actually been sudden. The lusting in Ed's eyes had always been a temptation to Paula. Her body commanded every thought in her mind. It had been that way for much too long to turn off the desires, the needs.

Paula slowly stood, moaning, went into the

kitchen. It was three in the morning. She opened the cupboard and pulled down the half-filled bottle of vodka. Her hangover needed soothing; it needed release.

Paula poured herself a stiff shot of liquor, gulped it down, and then felt a churning sickness bubble up from her stomach.

Suddenly, without warning, Paula doubled up, her guts erupting out through her trembling, convulsing lips.

How long she was caught up in the sickness, Paula didn't know. She was trembling when it was over, sicker still from the vile smell that attacked her.

Struggling to her feet, Paula rushed out of the kitchen, hurried across the apartment toward the bedroom. Once there, she fell exhausted on the bed. Almost immediately consciousness ebbed away.

* * * * * * *

Ed Beckerman had called Peter into his office and there was a stilted heavy atmosphere that reached out and choked around him. The man's eyes were like steel, cold.

Ed Beckerman had a cigar clamped between his teeth and he leaned back in his large swivel chair, silently brooding at Peter. It was the only word Peter could think of to describe what the man was doing.

Finally Ed Beckerman said in a low, slow speaking voice, "Peter, you have a good future with this firm, if you play your cards right. Mr. Kelbore likes you...likes your approach. He'll be in this afternoon to talk to you—to listen to your ideas. Now, I want to warn you about this. What you say will be...well, on your own neck. You aren't sticking out my neck. So play it cool if you want to be around here for very long."

"Did you hire me to play it cool? Or play it smart?"

"Be a winner. That's all I expect! Winners stay around. And I admit you've being tossed a big whale, a bull of a problem...without much seasoning on the job!"

"Well, you hired me to add something to the firm—not take away from it! So I'll do my best."

"I suppose that's all I can ask."

The man frowned, leaned forward and then snapped out, almost blasting at Peter: "What's this I hear about you and Paula?"

The words startled Peter. For a moment he wasn't sure what to say; what was expected from him. There was a glaring expression in Beckerman's eyes which almost frightened him.

"Well, it's...just that we've seen each other a—"

"I know that! I don't like it!" Beckerman snapped angrily, waving his cigar in the air in front of his face. "I don't like it at all!"

Peter was speechless. If anything, he had thought it would have been good for him to see Paula. Plus the woman was a mature adult, living her own life—and wasn't dependant on anybody.

"I don't understand!" Peter finally managed.

"Well...I don't like complicating things. My sister-in-law...well, you see she's a problem—as I imagine you've guessed and...well, we don't like to get things messy—and anyway, it might complicate things here at the office. People might get to talking—thinking we were—well," he smiled, but the movement of his lips was forced and set, "we don't want them thinking I'm playing favorites, and that's what they'll think!"

"Don't you think it's between Paula and myself?" Peter offered in a careful voice, so there would be plenty of room to back down.

"You let me handle Paula!" Beckerman announced angrily.

"Okay," Peter said embarrassed. In a way he felt strangely relieved.

It wasn't until he got to his office and a phone call from Paula came through that he felt the relief slither away.

"Peter, can I see you?" she asked desperately. He thought quickly, then said: "I'm pretty tied up right now, Paula."

"When, tonight?" she pushed in a rasping voice.

"I don't think so...I'm tied up tonight, Paula."

There was a stony silence and then she said: "Well, then, I'll call tomorrow, okay, Peter?"

He hesitated then said: "Fine, you do that."

You're a damned coward, he thought as he hung up the phone. A moment later he buzzed for his secretary and said: "How about tonight, Ann?"

"What about tonight?" she countered coyly.

"Dinner...the works?"

"Fine."

The connection broke, and Peter sat there for a few moments and thought about Paula, then about Ann, comparing them, feeling a wonderful joy that the comparison favored Ann.

* * * * * *

106

It was three and Kelbore was waiting nervously in Beckerman's office. He was thinking about the young man who was going to take over his account. There was a feeling of mixed reactions about Scott.

Kelbore was a good judge of men—or at least he thought of himself as such. He had noticed that there had been a lack of excitement in Peter's face after the film. Some people were like that, Kelbore realized—all too many, in his world..

As the office door opened suddenly, Kelbore's attention reverted to the present and he stood, extended his hand towards Peter Scott. Ed Beckerman, who was sitting behind his desk, stayed seated, said: "I want this young man to tell you exactly what he has in mind."

Kelbore wasn't deaf to the accent on the word "he." Beckerman was putting all the agency's blame or lack of blame on the new man.

He smiled as he looked at Peter Scott. A clean young man, that much he had to say.

"Well I looked at the report you sent me yesterday, Peter. The only thing I want to know is do you want the Kelbore name on the brand?"

"No! I don't think that's necessary. The only thing I'm trying to prove is that you'll sell more whiskey with a new approach. You'll be developing a new line at the same time." Peter sat down in the only other vacant chair in the room. He looked relaxed and in control of the situation, but Kelbore could guess that he was more nervous than he appeared. Obviously his job was on the line.

For a moment Kelbore considered the situation and then finally nodded. "Okay, I'll give you the chance you want. But I'll be honest with you, son your neck is stuck out. If this thing proves…well, off base, I'll have to suggest some changes and…" He shrugged his shoulders and then smiled warmly. "But I guess you aren't worrying about that, are you?"

"No, sir," Peter Scott said quickly. "I'm convinced!"

* * * * * * *

Ed Beckerman had called Paula that afternoon, and there was nothing she could do but comply to his demands. At first she'd said: "What's the use?"

He countered with: "Paula, you wouldn't want Diana to know what happened between us, would you?"

For a moment she was merely silent, thinking over that last statement. Things obviously were crumbling between Peter and herself. She doubted it was Peter's idea, and she was determined to do anything possible to make sure that Ed Beckerman didn't get between them.

"Maybe I'd like to talk to you, too," Paula finally said

She decided on the line of action to take with Ed Beckerman. He was threatening to tell Diana about the bed games they'd played—that was obviously a bluff. But Paula had one hell of a bluff on her side of the coin. A bluff she wasn't afraid to back up. Either Ed Beckerman kept out of her way with Peter and herself, or she'd cut him cold—cut off all games.

A strange light brightened Paula's eyes; it was almost as if some insane emotion had burned hot in her brain.

Slowly she stood and went into the bedroom to get dressed. Ed Beckerman was making an afternoon stop-off at her apartment before going home. This was the kind of game he was in the habit of making with any woman who happened to be his immediate bed partner. A quickie after work before facing his cold wife.

Paula decided she had a few surprises waiting for him.

//<u>Chapter Thirteen</u>\\

Paula lay back on the bed next to the man. It had been a long, angry session. Her body ached and her mind was sick inside. But this was the time to strike.

She turned, faced Ed Beckerman.

"Exactly what do you expect to gain by this little situation?" she demanded nastily.

Beckerman jerked up, his eyes wide, his mouth hard lines. "You think I like this?" he demanded.

It was Paula's turn to be surprised; really surprised. "I can't understand you, Ed," she told the man. "You surely must know that I hate your guts. What the hell are you getting out of this? Some kind of kick?"

His eyes lowered and for a moment he was silent. Finally he said in a slow, low voice:

"Paula, I don't know what's happening to me. I've never done anything like this before and—" Paula laughed in his face. "Never done anything like this? Hell, you've been banging that secretary of yours...and a few other women I won't mention!"

"I didn't mean that...I meant a situation like *this*! Before it was something that both people wanted. I...I don't know what's happening to me." For a long moment he looked desperately into her eyes and she felt suddenly sorry for him.

110

"You know it can't last…it can't continue. Why don't you divorce Diana—rather than cheat on her?" Paula suggested, looking evenly at the man, and knowing exactly why he wouldn't divorce her.

"Because I love her, regardless!" Beckerman admitted.

With that, Paula slipped off the bed and hurried into the bathroom.

She was shaking. She could hardly believe what had happened. What was far worse was the fact that she'd been fooling herself. It would have been easy to call it off right from the beginning, if she'd really played it smart. If she'd argued with herself like she'd just done. If she'd merely looked at herself honestly. The fact was that she'd wanted to sleep with Ed Beckerman—she had wanted the excuse.

Paula was suddenly sick of herself, sick inside, sick of the stomach. All day she'd been drinking too much

She slipped down onto the bathroom floor and sat there, staring blankly into space.

* * * * * * *

Diana knew that she was about to break the seams. Every since her husband had called that afternoon and said he would be home late from work, she had felt the depression eat away at her

For the first time in her life, Diana was beginning to face the facts that her husband wasn't being completely honest with her. Maybe it was rationalization, she didn't know. She needed an excuse to do exactly what Paula had suggested.

Diana told the maid that she was going to a movie She had dressed in a green sweater and tight-fitting skirt. It wasn't smart to have a drink at home, but she took enough money in her purse to take care of that.

Diana drove to the first bar she could find, parked, and then went into the dark saloon. Stepping up to the bar, Diana ordered two martinis. After they had been consumed, she sat there thinking about herself and about her life.

Yet the problem had kept so vivid in her brain. She was losing her husband and there wasn't anything she could do about it by just standing still. Either she gave up, or she made some fumbling effort to correct or change her situation.

Diana left the bar, returned to her car and then drove down to the middle of town toward the west end, where some of the cheaper saloons were located. She was just high enough to have the courage to go through with what she knew was necessary. Or at least believe it was going to be possible.

Once sitting in a small, cheap bar, music sounding from the jukebox in the corner, Diana's courage weakened. She ordered a double martini and finished it off as fast as possible.

Then Diana ordered another, and when it came she sipped from it. The liquor was beginning to feed its way through her nervous system.

Diana headed toward Paula's. She was just bringing the car to a stop when she saw Ed Beckerman stepping out of Paula's apartment, closing the door behind him.

Panic flushed over her. For a startled, dazed moment the world shattered, exploded away, and reality didn't exist anymore.

She was driving, fast, down the highway toward Kenmore City. How she'd gotten there, Diana didn't know. It seemed much like a movie cut. One moment she'd been in front of Paula's apartment and then the next moment she was driving along the highway.

It was the sound of a police siren that jarred her thoughts to reality. Suddenly a cop was speeding along side her.

"Pull over, lady!" the man ordered nastily.

* * * * * * *

Ed Beckerman was just getting into his apartment when the phone rang. He had been driving for a long time, thinking about his life, about his wife, about everything that had led him to this place, this time.

It was finished between Paula and himself. He knew that much. He was glad, in a way. Now that he had thought it over, he knew that what Paula had said had been true. He was a no good bastard. What he'd done to Diana, by cheating on her, was all too cruel. He hated himself for that part of his life; for that part of himself.

Ed picked up the receiver and then said: "Yes?"

"Mr. Beckerman?"

"Yes?"

"We have your wife here at the station—in Kenmore City. She was picked up on a drunken driving charge. I think you better come down right away," the voice said over the receiver.

For a moment Ed Beckerman stood there, dazed, unable to believe what he'd heard. Diana never really drank that much. He couldn't understand what had happened.

Then another thought suddenly suggested itself to him: maybe he didn't want to understand.

"I'll be right down!" Ed announced, slamming the receiver on the hook. He stood there, sweating, sick inside.

What was happening to them? What in the world was happening to their lives, to their world?

Sick, he rushed out of the apartment and got into his car. It was well over thirty minutes before he parked in front of the police station in Kenmore City.

Some time later, as Ed Beckerman was driving his wife toward their home, he asked: "What happened?"

"Didn't the police tell you?" she demanded coldly from her far side of the car.

The night was cold and chilly, like her voice; dark and foreboding.

"They said you were picked up on a drunk driving charge—that's all I know!" It was the first exchange since he had escorted her out of the police station and into his car.

"I'm going to divorce you, Ed," Diana suddenly blurted out.

Ed Beckerman suddenly slammed on his brakes. The car twisted and spun around, the back end whipping into the side of a telephone post and slamming to a stop.

For a moment the two said nothing.

Then Diana blurted out: "What the hell are you trying to do!"

"I'm sorry! The car..." His voice was shaky, his hands unsteady. "What do you mean you're getting a divorce?"

"I should kill you for...for...what I saw! What were you doing at Paula's?" she cried.

All Ed could do was sit there, stunned, unable to say anything. What could he say? What possibly could he do?

Sick inside, he faced the front of the car, started the engine and then headed down the highway, toward home.

They didn't say anything more that night.

Ed went into the study, a bottle of liquor in his hand and sat in the comfortable overstuffed chair. All he could think about was that his marriage was finished, completely ruined, and only because of his hunger, his frantic search for something that suddenly didn't seem important at all.

//<u>Chapter Fourteen</u>\\

That night when Ann Fenneran invited Peter Scott into her apartment for a nightcap, he felt an excited flutter rush up through him.

It was strange how he was beginning to feel toward Ann Fenneran. They really hardly knew each other, but there was already a feeling of having known her for a much longer time. As if they had been friends for years.

What the hell was he doing? From one woman to another! He thought about Paula, about Joanne. It all seemed like some fantastic dream. And here he was with Ann Fenneran; and there wasn't the least doubt in his mind that he could make love to her.

Without knowing why, Peter didn't like the idea of playing around with Ann. He desired her, but didn't want to use her.

For a long moment he puzzled over that thought.

Had he been merely playing a practicing game with Joanne? Or had that merely been the way it had started—the excuse—and then he'd gotten really interested, a really serious?

How puzzling and confusing the mind and motives and passions can be, Peter told himself.

"Boy," Ann exclaimed, "are you in a think-think!"

Peter jarred himself out of the mental wanderings. "I was just wondering about...well, people—the way they are with each other. You know—the young kid who goes out with a girl, and thinks, he'll just see how far things can go—just to get experience—what a real rotten attitude—a sick attitude!"

Ann nodded. "But it goes both ways. The girls will say—if the boy wants my company he can pay for it! A big dinner. Show. You name it. But it'll cost him. So—it goes both ways."

"And what about adults?" Peter suggested squeezing her closer for a moment.

She looked up into his eyes, searching, questioning, then said: "That depends on the people and just how they feel about each other—and about life—and about their future. What they are looking for. I'm wondering about you, Peter."

The last part of her statement startled him. "What are you wondering?" His eyes went instinctively to her neckline.

"Okay. About you again. That company eats up bright young men. And if they want a good life, a good family life, it can be difficult—if they drive too hard," Ann announced seriously

"Why the pitch? What are you after?"

"After you...maybe," she smiled in a mocking, teasing way "Maybe just that I want to know exactly where you are going."

"I thought we'd been through that already."

"Yes, but it didn't tell me enough." This time she slid her arms around his neck as she smiled up into his eyes "Peter I like you a lot," she breathed, her full dimpled lips only a breath away from his.

For a moment he was able to control the fantastic screaming in his ears, and then he jerked her against him and the screaming stopped.

They kissed passionately, straining together, then slowly she slipped back, away. Her eyes probed his, for a long time.

Finally Ann said "I don't know what you have in mind, Peter but—"

"To be blunt, I want to make love to you, Ann," he told her.

Strangely she said: "Why?"

It was the kind of question almost impossible to answer. Oh, normally, he might have been able to come up with a good, light retort, but instead, he found himself stumbling mentally over his answer.

Why did he want to make love to her? Just to have some kicks? Just for fun and games. Just because this was another woman, another thrill, another night of passion?

These were new, disturbing thoughts to Peter. Partly because it had been such a long haul with Joanne, and he'd been able to convince himself it was because of love, and that he would marry her someday. Now Joanne was distant, a thing of his past.

And what was his present? Making love to any willing woman? The thought depressed him.

Peter looked at Ann, said: "I think maybe I'd better leave."

For a moment she hesitated and seemed about to tell him to stay. Then, just as suddenly as he had moved, she nodded. "Yes, maybe...maybe it would be better."

When Peter had gone, Ann stood there looking at

the door, puzzled, shaken by what had happened.

Yet, she wondered, maybe he knew exactly what he was doing. Maybe he was playing a cool, sure game with her—maybe he was so sure of himself he was attempting to wind her completely around his fingers. Maybe it was a damned fool thing getting involved with her boss. Quite dangerous for both of them. Maybe it should be cut right to the quick—and quick! Before things got out of control.

* * * * * * *

Peter didn't drive directly home that evening. What was happening to him?

Everything had seemed so simple at first. Go out and get a job, start a new life. Then—and only then—get married, when things were solid and secure. Then Paula had stormed in. And now Ann Fenneran.

Why hadn't he made love to her? Why hadn't he pulled her into his arms once more, and then a little later, lifted her into his arms, and carried her into the bedroom? That was what he had wanted to do.

The only thing which had stopped him had been that question about why he wanted to make love to Ann. It was a casual, normal question, in a way. But it had jarred him, had cut deep, revealing a confusion of thought he hadn't been fully aware existed.

Peter realized he had parked on a side street, totally unaware of having done so.

He started the car, and a little later found himself parked outside Ann's apartment. How long he sat there, looking up at the window of her living room, he didn't know. But finally he started the car again and headed toward his own apartment.

* * * * * * *

Diana Beckerman woke with a throbbing hang-over. As she lay in bed, drowned in pain it was hard to believe what had happened the night before. The anguish, the pain, the hurt moved its way through her.

Where was her life, now? What was going to happen to her—and her children?

And all because of pride, and because of sex and her fear of being frigid. Was sex the most important thing in the world? Was it the beginning and the end of all things? Without it, could a marriage really survive?

Those thoughts drove her though the next couple of hours. This time, when she went to the phone, her mind was made up.

"Is Doctor Gordon there? "she asked in a shaking voice.

The nurse hesitated, said: "He's busy right now."

"This is Diana Beckerman—it's important..."

Silence for a moment and then, "I'll see."

A few moments later a deep, mannish voice sounded through the receiver.

"Yes?" Doctor Gordon inquired.

"I...I want to...see a doctor—a...person who could help me...about my...about something personal!" she blurted out.

The doctor's smooth voice said: "Is it an emotional problem?"

"Something like that," she told him. "Isn't there somebody you could send me to?"

"Well, I'd like to see you, first, Diana."

120

Panic set in. She couldn't talk to Doctor Gordon. He knew her too well. It would be too embarrassing. Then she gripped the receiver harder, determined to see it through, this time.

"Could you...see me today?"

The doctor checked and then said there was time about 3:15 in the afternoon.

As she hung up the phone, Diana was sweating, shaking.

For a moment only she was tempted to call the whole thing off. Then she remembered her children, and she remembered her husband. Something had to be done. It might not be too late to save their marriage. Yet, it might not be too late.

//<u>Chapter Fifteen</u>\\

Paula had called him up at the office, and a feeling of emotional release had caught hold of Peter at hearing her voice.

He had made arrangements to see her after dinner at her apartment for cocktails.

It was eight in the evening when he arrived. She had dressed in a red sheath, which showed, off her body in a blatantly seductive manner. It was a calculated move to seduce him.

"Hello," she greeted, closing the door behind him. She looked at him and then suddenly slipped closer, her arms slipping around his neck. "I'm so glad you…accepted."

They kissed. It was an automatic kiss, without much emotion in it.

A little later, as they were sitting on the sofa, listening to music, sipping drinks, Paula said:

"I talked to Ed about you, Peter."

He stiffened. "What about?"

She was silent for a moment, hesitating, as if uncertain what words to pick in answer to that question.

Peter offered: "He didn't want you to see me, did he?"

"Well, he won't get in our way any longer."

"Paula," he said, turning and looking into her eyes. "I don't know what you are after...if its mere kicks—for awhile, no strings attached...well, that will work itself out. If it's something else..."

She frowned, leaned close and then caressed his cheek with her lips. "Do we have to talk, Peter?"

"No...but—"

"But...what?"

"I shouldn't be here. It's really a mistake. My motives were...to be frank...rather selfish. I came, merely because you're hot and sexy and willing—I was depressed and—"

"Isn't that enough?" she offered in a strangely tense voice, as if she were holding back some emotion.

He shrugged and pulled her hungrily into his arms.

In the semi-darkness of the bedroom, their bodies surged harder together and she felt the strength of him pressing eagerly against her own body. The thrill inched over every nerve. Her body screamed for his, for the feel of him, for the delicious strength making them one throbbing unit on the bed.

Finally he slipped out of her arms and she took that as her cue to undress. The nervous action of her fingers on the zipper of her dress revealed all the signs to Paula. She was hot as hell for this man. So desperately hungrily for him that she had already begun to lose all her control, all her pride, all those things which had taken years to develop. And because of that, Paula was convinced, beyond all reason, that she was now completely and madly in love with Peter. Where before she had been sure—now she knew it would be impossible to fight it any longer—to argue with herself. From this moment on Paula knew she would do anything possible to win this man, to have him all for herself.

Something was happening to Paula, and she was only aware of the surface change. It was the inner change which would be dangerous. For only a fluttering moment that bothered her, then she focused on the man as he stared hungrily at her.

* * * * * * *

Peter hurriedly undressed. By the time he was ready to move to the bed, Paula was already stretched out, waiting for him.

And even while making love to Paula's lush body, his thoughts turned to Ann Fenneran.

All day it had been difficult working, difficult to keep his mind on what he was supposed to be doing. Every time he would see Ann, he had felt the wild desire to pull her into his arms and smother her lips with kisses. It was different from the way that Paula had affected him, because of that he was frightened, terrified of Ann.

What was so terrifying was the fact that he was frightened of Ann. He'd just gotten free from one woman—was he getting serious with another?

"Oh, God, Peter!" Paula's voice cried out in anguish and pleasure as she tensed up against him.

The sound of that voice, so full of passion, so full of excitement, jarred him back to what he was doing.

When the woman's hands reached over toward him and caressed over his body, Peter felt a vague sense of displeasure, even though it was impossible to stop the caresses. Again, like previously, he found himself possessed by the sexual power of Paula's demanding passions.

It was a long, long time before they broke away from each other's embrace.

A little later he was driving home.

He was just undressing when the phone rang. Startled, Peter was almost tempted to ignore the call. *Who the hell could be calling him at this hour?*

Picking up the phone, he said in a tight, angry voice: "Yes?"

"Oh, thank God, Peter." It was his mother.

"What's wrong?" He was alarmed by the thick sound of his mother's voice.

"It's Joanne. Something terrible's happened!"

There was a sobbing sound and then suddenly the gruff voice of his father sounded over the receiver.

"Get over here!" he snapped nastily. "And get fast. You've killed Jo!"

The next minutes were a blurring red haze to Peter Scott. His father's cruel words kept ringing over and over again in his ears. He was vaguely aware of driving, but didn't remember getting into the car.

Then suddenly he was in the large home in which he'd lived most of his life.

His mother was crying. His father's face, ruddy, hard, eyes flaring with angry fury.

Ross Scott was saying: "She was killed in an auto accident. But...believe me...it was your fault. Ever since you broke off with her...she was over last night—and...we talked...and she drank. She told us things—and, well..."

His father's face hardened even more. "She was pregnant!"

Everything exploded for Peter. Some how he was

out of the house, walking. Then it was morning and he was standing outside Paula Martin's apartment. A moment later, through the continuing haze that had attacked him, Peter found himself banging on the apartment door.

Then Paula was in his arms, and he was sobbing, like a little boy, like a frightened kid, unable to control himself. He wasn't even really aware, or caring, who Paula was.

Sometime during that awful haze he found himself drinking straight whiskey. Then a little later he felt the lushness of a feminine body pressing against his. And he made love, through the anguish, through the dazed drunkenness, to this voluptuous willing body that gave itself freely to him.

To Peter it was merely action, escape, running, going down a dark tunnel away from the reality of the world. The reality that Joanne was dead, that she had carried his child to death—that his world was crumbling—even when it had been building to a good solid future.

He couldn't escape the terrible thought that if he'd known about Joanne being pregnant, that he would have been trapped with a woman he didn't love, he didn't want to think about that because it was too horrible.

He merely felt, drank and experienced.

It happened so fast, without warning, without any thing that could cushion the blow to him.

He merely took Paula, felt the softness of her. And tried not to think about anything else.

* * * * * * *

To Paula this was a strange and wonderful turn of events. She would never have thought that Peter would come to her in a moment of need. She had thrilled to his outburst of emotion, the flood of words, and the meanings that they meant to her.

It had been a tragic thing that had happened; that she wasn't happy about. But that Peter had come to her was another matter.

Now, in his arms, Paula was sure of herself and the future hold she would have on Peter Scott's life.

//**Chapter Sixteen**\\

For Peter Scott the next days were a wild, I savagely horrible torment. He couldn't keep his mind on his work, he couldn't think about anything other than the mess he'd made out of Joanne's life. It didn't seem possible that she was gone. Why had she died? Maybe it had merely been an accident, maybe it was something else—he would never know. That reality was totally demoralizing.

And the immediate days after her death had crushed him completely. They had been a tragic agony. Depression had set in. The thought of having been a father—almost—was another wound that would scar over but never go away. The funeral was a blur of emotional pain, numbed by a lot of drinking. His own confusion about what he actually felt was overwhelming. Losing Jo was a terrible event in his life; something he would never completely get over. They had been together for so long, shared so much, and had, during most of that time planned on a life together. Now that was all shattered, blown away and he felt a mixture of relief along with the horrid empty sadness. But it was more like the ending of one chapter of his life and the opening of a new one, the slate clean. And he felt terribly guilty about that fact. A dear friend had died, and that was, in itself, horrid, painful and ripped a huge gap from his life; but it relieved him to experience the future with a new freedom that hadn't been possible while Jo was there to claim him as her own.

Yet every time he would think about her a hard lump would form in his throat and tears would rush to his eyes.

It was Ann Fenneran who first brought up the subject between them.

"I heard about Miss Nestor's accident," she said one afternoon, a couple of days after he had learned about it. "I'm terribly sorry."

For a moment Peter merely stared in space, blandly. Each night, after work, he had gone blindly to Paula's apartment where they had drunk themselves silly and found complete escape in each other's bodies. It was the only escape that made it possible for him to continue. Blind, unemotional, savagely engaged sex.

He looked into Ann's eyes and for a moment the flickering of desire welled there. Then he shrugged off the thought. He had no business getting involved with any woman. He shouldn't even be with Paula, but couldn't help himself there. Peter was frightened for his emotional sanity.

That night, in Paula's lush arms, Peter's thoughts turned to Ann Fenneran, and he wondered about her, he wondered what it would be like to be holding her in his arms. The thought puzzled him.

It was puzzling, because he had no business thinking about Ann.

The next morning his throat was burning up, his eyes blurry, and when he staggered into the office, still half drunk, Ann looked up from her desk, a frown played on her forehead.

"Peter...what's wrong?" she asked, alarmed.

"Nothing...a hangover," he mumbled, starting past her desk.

Ann helped him into the inner office and closed the door behind him. "What's bothering you, Peter?" she inquired gently. "I mean; you said it was over between you and—"

"Don't!" he fairly shouted at Ann.

She recoiled as if slapped. For a moment her face flushed, either in embarrassment or anger, he didn't know which.

He said: "I'm sorry. Maybe you're right."

"About what?"

"About me...I'm hitting it pretty hard." Impulsively Peter found himself saying: "Could I see you...tonight?"

He frowned at his own statement. *What would Paula think?* To hell with Paula. He had to talk to somebody—somebody who would understand. He was quite well aware of the fact that Paula was using the situation to her own advantage. He didn't think she even cared a damned. She was a selfishly involved female in heat.

"Sure, Peter," Ann said. "My place? Dinner?" she offered.

* * * * * * *

Diana Beckerman sat in the living room, waiting for her husband to come home. She had downed a couple of stiff whiskies and already felt a dull glowing band around her head. She would need the strength the drinks.

That day she had been to Doctor Elliott Simpson, the man who Doctor Gordon had sent her to. It was her second visit. Dr. Simpson was a tall, large man with a thick mustache and probing, deep-set eyes. When he had ushered her into his small inner office the first time, she had been nervous and out of sorts. It just didn't seem possible to talk to this stranger. But the moment the door had been closed and he had started for his dark highly polished desk, Diana knew that there was no backing out, now.

Dr. Simpson had sat and indicated that he expected her to do the same, in the chair opposite his, across the desk from him.

"No couch...unless you want one." He smiled and leaned over the desk to light her

"Dr. Gordon says you have some problems," he smiled, relaxing in the chair. "You know, from what I've been told about your problem, I don't see why we can't come right to the point and tell you that there's nothing really extremely different about you than many other women. You'd be surprised how many women come to me and need this kind of help. Tell me, how do you feel about your husband?"

The question had come so quickly, out of left field, that she'd answered instantly with "I love him very much—regardless."

Then she just started blabbering. The words just flowed, almost disconnected. Thoughts, memories, all about her background, but mostly about her and Ed. Finally the hour was up and he simply nodded, saying that she should return in a couple of days. "Just consider this:

"Think of your husband as a person with a problem and think of him as a person who loves you. If you
look at it in that way—and realize that he loves you—
and I'm assuming that this is what you believe, then
you have to face him as a person who loves you and
wants to understand you."

They made the appointment for this afternoon and
that session was far more to the point. He came right to
it in the first minutes she stepped into his office, and
sat in the chair. He hesitated for only a moment before
saying:

"Mrs. Beckerman, you told me that you found little
pleasure in your husband's love making. You also told
me about your mother and some of your own attitudes
about life and sex. Now could I tell you something
about the reality of life and sex and love?"

She merely nodded, suddenly embarrassed. The
other day they had talked a long, long time, yet she
still felt the embarrassment.

"For centuries it was believed that sex was merely
for reproduction, and that women were not supposed
to have any sexual feelings. In some societies women
are circumcised so that they don't have any pleasure
during the relationship. But in our modern day life, it
has been quite bluntly brought to light that women are
no different from men in their basic desires...only in
that it takes longer to spark that desire. And you are
built differently and your bodies are created for a different function. Men need release; you women have to
be very careful, for you could end up pregnant under
the wrong circumstances. So there are built-in safe-
guards. But that doesn't have anything to do with the
fact that you're just as able to enjoy sex and to achieve

132

orgasm. Yet, what you need to consider, Mrs. Beckerman, is things have changed since you grandmother's day. And don't kid yourself, they enjoyed sex, too…they just didn't talk about those kind of things. Now, today, information is becoming far more open and extensive. We know differently today. We're learning more all the time. Sex is for love, for pleasure, and for having children. But there are still people—much like yourself—who believe differently, or rather, were raised to believe differently.

He was silent for some moments, studying her thoughtfully. Finally he said, "I want you to talk to Mr. Beckerman and then have him come in with you the next time. If he really loves you and if he wants your marriage to continue, he will come, believe me. I know from experience. There have been many cases that were far worse than yours. Cases which didn't seem to have any hope of being saved…and with a little work and understanding, things worked out."

Silence followed until he asked: "Will you do this for me? Talk to your husband?"

She had nodded yes.

And so, now she was waiting for her husband, slightly drunk. In such a condition it might be possible to talk to him—it might be possible to come right out and say all the things that were necessary to say in order to save their marriage.

To Diana Beckerman it was her only and last chance.

Then a key fit into the front door and Ed Beckerman stepped into the hallway. He moved into the living room, saw Diana sitting there, waiting.

"I want to talk to you, Ed," Diana announced.

"What's there to talk about?" he demanded nastily.

"Our marriage," she offered, sitting up straight and looking directly into his eyes.

"I thought you were going to get a divorce" he told her.

Diana shook her head slowly. Things had been pretty horrible the last days, since she had made that foolish announcement. They had lived together, but in a silent cold war attitude.

"Ed...I don't want to divorce you...saw a doctor to-day...he's trying to help me."

"Oh, great!" he exploded, glaring at her. "What will a doctor do for you?"

"Please, give me a chance! I'm willing to forget the past—start over—can't we?" She stood, stepped across the room toward him. Then she moved close. "Please, Ed, there are so many things we have to talk about...so many things to make it possible to keep our marriage going—to give us a future—if for nothing other than the children. But not for the children alone—but for you and me!"

For a moment the man was stiff and cold, outwardly. Then slowly a sigh broke from his lips, he said: "Okay...let's give it a try but from the beginning." Then his voice broke and he crushed her to him. "Oh, God, I love you Diana. I've never really loved any other woman...please...oh, please forgive me!"

//<u>Chapter Seventeen</u>\\

They were sipping cocktails. The coziness of Ann Fenneran's apartment was striking and he felt strangely relaxed for the first time in days. As Peter looked at Ann, studied her features, it was hard to convince himself that this was the same girl who worked for him at the office. It was the first time he was so sharply aware of her as a person, as a woman. And she was lovely, seductive, delightful company. Before, it had been, he now realized, a matter of action and reaction, automatic and without thought. And the last days, weeks, had been a horrid nightmare.

This was a woman he could talk to, and somehow he knew she would be tenderly understanding; caring. This was a woman a man could easily become very close to, a woman who might become special, some day—at least as a dear friend. And he needed a friend. And he needed somebody who could be special; even if just for the moment.

Why should he be seeing Ann this way now? he wondered, vaguely annoyed by the thought.

He remembered Joanne Nestor and what had happened to her with great emotional pain; that simply wouldn't go away.

The last weeks had been an emotional challenge,

and a bloody blur. He had managed to walk through the first days, then slowly things become more orderly and focused. Work had helped. The lonely nights were less painful and now with the prospect of escaping into the arms of other women would help take some of the anguish away, numb the hurt wounds, sooth the heeling process into place.

Women like Ann were there to help him through the next months. He felt comfortable with her.

Ann was a special woman who seemed to care about others, and seemed to like him. Focusing on her was a positive move away from the past and towards his future life, wherever it might take him. That was a start in the right direction.

His face worked into a frown, the lines around his eyes becoming more intense. Ann leaned closer, patted his hand.

"I know...it must be difficult," she said in a soft, gentle voice.

Suddenly the words which he had wanted to tell her started to flow out. It was as if somebody had all at once taken control of his vocal cords. His mind was aware of everything that was happening around him, as if detached. He watched the expression on Ann's face and the actions of her eyes as he spoke.

"We were pretty serious, you know. Very serious for a long time. But I never could quite make it—I mean...get married. I don't know exactly why. But I think it was because I wasn't that much in love with Joanne. I learned the other day when dad told me about the accident that she had been visiting them...and that she'd been pregnant and..." His voice faltered then. He lowered his eyes. "I shouldn't have told you that..."

"That's all right, Peter," Ann told him in a soft, but firm voice. Then after a moment of silence, said: "You blame yourself, don't you?"

He merely nodded.

"I don't know...it's none of my business, but I can't see how you can blame yourself. If I'd been in that position I would have gone to you...I would have told you the truth—maybe she planned on doing so...in time she probably would have. In any case...it's a horrible thing, but you have to live, Peter. I've seen you these last days...you don't seem to care about anything!"

"I know...I have to live..." he murmured so softly that he wasn't even quite sure she had heard him.

"Everybody has to face life, Peter...and make the best out of it. This isn't a nice thing to say—but it's the truth. The past is gone. You can't go back and start all over—you can't erase what has happened. But you can...well, make the most of the future." She laughed nervously. "Listen to me! Doctor Fenneran, at your service, sir!"

Her blue eyes twinkled brightly. Her hand reached out and touched his. "You can't let this ruin you. You have a good future ahead of you—and there's no reason why you should throw it away because of guilt about something that actually wasn't your fault. An accident is an accident. You don't know what she might have done—if it hadn't happened. Accept it...and now, how about dinner?"

Her hand squeezed his. And in her eyes he read something which startled him, it was an open call of one woman toward the man she is violently interested in. Just a momentarily flicker which veiled over.

As Ann stood and walked into the kitchen, Peter found his mind automatically comparing her to all the other women he had known—especially to Joanne and Paula. There was a difference, which was strong and wonderful. Joanne had been a little girl, Paula was a bitch in heat. Ann was a mature, intelligent woman, who had been on her own for some time, who looked at life the way it was and accepted it.

When she returned, his eyes dipped to the cut of her neckline, which gave an intriguing, but reserved suggestion of breasts. The brown dress clung to her body with just a respectable amount of sexuality, without being overly forward. Attractive, but neither girlish nor bitchy.

They ate mainly in silence. And when dinner was finished, Ann suggested a walk.

"Get some fresh air," she offered.

A little later they were walking along the darkened street, hand in hand, saying nothing. Yet there was a wonderfully relaxed mood about what they were doing—a wonderful simplicity which was all too appealing.

This was the kind of thing that a husband and wife might do. The action which was casual and friendly, without tension, without the universal game of "dating" or "seducing" being a part of it. When they returned to her apartment a little later, Ann fixed some coffee and they sat in the kitchen, at the small table there, waiting for the coffee to get ready.

A short lock of hair fell over Ann's forehead, and with an embarrassed move of her hand she tried to sweep it away. But it returned into position.

"Leave it, it's attractive that way," Peter told her.

His hand folded over hers. He didn't think thoughts of seduction. He didn't think thoughts of wild erotic bed games. Oddly he merely thought about Ann, wondered what was going on in that brain of hers, wondered what she thought of him. Most of all, he was simply enjoying being with her—without anything else being necessary.

"Ann," he finally said, "you don't know how much this has meant to me."

She merely smiled.

"I mean it." Then he asked. "I still can't understand why you never got married."

An embarrassed flush worked up her cheeks. It was most attractive and feminine.

"I was never asked by the right man!"

The coffee was ready then, and she hurriedly got up, as if the conversation had embarrassed her too much.

He watched her pouring the coffee and felt that wave of contented relaxation. It was just like they were in love and married. So much like a man's wife pouring coffee for him. And with that thought came the question: what kind of wife would Ann Fenneran make? The answer was simple: she's going to make one hell of a good wife to a lucky enough man to get her.

As she sat down again opposite him, Peter found his thoughts more and more centering around the idea of Ann as a wife. It was strange and completely out of place, considering what had happened to Joanne Nestor. And as he thought about her, he realized that suddenly the guilt was washed away. He did have a future to think about. A future that could be with a woman like this.

They drank their coffee in silence. When it was finished, Peter suddenly looked at his watch, said: "Maybe I'd better get going?" it was a question. He didn't want to leave.

"It's early," she pointed out.

They stood and went into the living room. Ann turned on the radio, until soft classical music was playing. He was standing next to her. As she turned, she was almost in his arms. They stood there for some time before he abruptly pulled her close. It seemed so natural, so beautiful. Just a gliding move that brought them together.

Their lips met and he thrilled to the softness of her lips. He thrilled to the excitement of her kiss. And just like that there was no turning back.

As they came out of the embrace, Ann was breathing hard. She stared at him for a moment and then hugged herself tighter to him again. "Would you think me too bold...*if* I said *I* wanted you to stay...late?"

The question was so touching, at that moment, to Peter, that he felt an emotional reaction to them. They were the words of a woman who wanted to be loved, but didn't want the man to lose respect for her.

"I never thought woman too bold. I...I like you a lot, Ann." He felt a shock wave hit him. He almost said that he loved her. But that was impossible. Completely and utterly impossible.

Ann pulled away and then smiling, said: "I'll be right back, Peter."

She disappeared into the bedroom. He heard her movements, subtle feminine movements which intrigued.

And as he listened, Peter felt his heart throbbing, his throat choking tight with emotion. What a wonderfully delightful woman, he thought, exciting to the idea of making love to her.

It was some time before he heard a whispered word.

"Peter..."

He didn't need a second call.

Peter walked to the bedroom door, opened it.

There was a small, dim light on the dresser across the room from the large double bed. It cast soft outlines on Ann's body, which was reposed on the bed, draped in a filmy blue negligee.

Never had he seen such a wonderful sight. There was a beauty that completely defied logic. It wasn't so much that Ann was the most beautiful or sexy woman in the world—but rather that she was a lovely, attractive female. And there was a simple beauty and perfection to her, as she lay there looking at him, waiting. Her body was a series of soft curves, swells, highlighted by the dim lighting. He watched the rising and falling of her breasts under the thin negligee, and thrilled silently to the sight.

"Ann," he said softly, stepping forward until he was standing over her. "Ann..." he breathed as he slipped down onto the bed beside her. His hand reached out and caressed her bare arm. "You are so beautiful." His throat was choked with emotion. But it was a new, all fired emotion he had never fully experienced before.

He wanted to hold her in his arms, he wanted to protect her, he wanted to tell her all the things he was feeling, all the emotions. He wanted to bathe her in loving words, caresses, in emotional waves to surround her very soul.

It was strange how suddenly it had come over him. There she had been all this time. There she had been, willing, soft, and wonderful. Waiting. But he was glad they had waited. All the past seemed to melt completely away and the only thing that mattered was the future; a future which would be his for the rest of his life. And now he wondered seriously if it might be possible that Ann would be an important part of that future.

"Ann...do you think it is possible for people to be...to...love another person you hardly know?" His lips were lowering slowly toward hers.

Instead of saying anything, her arms slipped around his neck and pulled him down against her lips.

The kiss, wonderful, soft, moist, affectionate, and then blending into hot passion. He felt her kiss open to his, the probe of her tongue. His hand reached instinctively to the softness of her breasts, feeling the supple fullness there, thrilling to the texture, to the nearness, to the woman.

As the kiss broke away, as his lips slid down to her throat, caressed the lobe of her ear, the words trembled out, naturally, honestly, "Oh, Ann, you are wonderful...so wonderful...could love you..."

She tensed against him, caressed his back. "Love me...for tonight, for tonight," she murmured softly in his ear.

And then they moved, they slipped closer. In the next moments he felt her hands gliding over him, helping him, until he was stripped, and after that, he caressed the top of her negligee away and lost all sense of reason, all sense of time, all sense of anything other than the nearness of this woman, her softness, her warmth, and beauty. And as his hands moved over her, his lips kissed her flesh, he felt the emotion well up through him, and wondered how it could be that he could feel such intense emotion for a woman he hardly

As his lips found the most sensitive, most fiery secrets of her body, as his caresses floated over her wonderful flesh, Peter Scott realized that he never wanted this to stop, never wanted to make love to any other woman. And startling as that was, he found it just as easy to accept.

When their bodies joined in the wonderful ecstasy of lovers, he was convinced of his feelings and of the future and of this woman. And afterwards, as they lay together in each other's arms, he found words breathing from his lips, words he would never have thought possible to say.

It was like some kind of beautiful concert, as they touched, caressed and found one another. Their actions were like a running intertwining of melodies that locked together into a perfect arrangement of such wonderful feelings that he was left almost numbed in the very pleasure of her. And with every wave of joyful ecstasy that smothered his total being, time and again, he found himself surrendering more and more to the rich sensation of being totally in love. He loved her. Totally. Completely.

Just like that.

"Ann oh, Ann...I never knew it could be like this, you're wonderful. I don't...I have never known any woman like you before. I...guess I'm..."

143

Her lips covered his for a moment and then she said:

"Peter...I'm a lonely woman...and I'm frightened of you...frightened of myself...I might get serious."

He laughed, cupped her face with his hands. "I'm already getting serious!"

They stared into each other's eyes and for a long time didn't say anything at all. But the communication was quite complete.

Like that it had happened. And this time he didn't doubt it in the least.

//<u>Chapter Eighteen</u>\\

And there was Paula to consider. Rather to handle. If possible.

It wasn't until the next day at work that Peter Scott realized that he couldn't just turn Paula off. He realized this with a sick, terrible feeling inside. What would Paula do? What would her reaction be?

He picked up the phone and then dialed her number. It was some time before she answered the ringing.

"Paula," he said, "I want to see you."

"When?" she asked, delighted.

"At noon?" he offered.

Ann came into the room at that time and heard the rest of the conversation, during which he mentioned Paula by name again.

Ann glared at him for a moment, then said:

"Well? I was wondering when she would come up again!"

Peter forced a smile. "I have to let her know about us."

"Oh?" Ann questioned, tightly.

"Please...don't you understand—I want to break it off with Paula—completely!" Peter announced.

Ann's expression softened and then she came around to his side of the desk. He stood and they embraced. "You really are serious, aren't you?"

"Is there any reason I shouldn't be?" he offered.

"No...I guess not." Then their lips met.

For a moment he enjoyed the kiss and then thought about Paula and wondered how the woman would take this new turn of events. He knew he owed Paula something more than the boot, with "Thanks, honey, but it's over!" written on it.

Paula wasn't the kind of woman to be turned off easy; if she wanted something—she went out and got it.

A shudder rushed over Peter. They arranged to meet at her place. Paula had insisted. He couldn't help thinking that things were going to get pretty hot—pretty violent, maybe.

When twelve noon came, Peter left quickly, stopped at the cocktail lounge downstairs in the lobby. Then after a martini, he headed for Paula's apartment.

* * * * * *

There had been something in Peter Scott's voice, which had frightened Paula. When she hung up the phone, she fought with the inner churning at the pit of her stomach.

All her life she had been searching for something, Paula realized. Something which she had found with Peter Scott. The very idea of losing him, now that things had gotten so good between them, terrified her.

She dressed in a house robe, putting on nothing underneath. Paula couldn't help thinking if things went bad, if it were true there had been something strange in Peter's voice, and it hadn't been her imagination then she'd need every weapon at her command. A naked body was the ultimate killer weapon.

When the doorbell rang, about twenty minutes after twelve, Paula quickly looked over the makeup on her face, opened the robe slightly, so that it hinted at the nakedness of her breasts, and then rushed to the door, opened it.

Peter walked in, quickly, avoiding any intimate embrace, stepped to the middle of the room, turned and faced her as she closed the door.

The look in the man's eyes told Paula all she needed to know. His voice merely stated what she had read in his eyes.

"Paula, I don't know exactly how to tell you this...but something has happened. Something vital and important to me...and...in a way it involves us—our relationship." He hesitated. "I might as well be brutally honest about this! I'm calling it off between us."

He stood there, as if ready for an outburst, as if knowing what her reaction would be.

Paula stared at him for a long moment before saying anything. Her voice was level and harsh even to her own ears as she said:" You can't, you know that, Peter. You know damned well you're just fooling yourself!"

With those words, Paula did the only thing possible to do, to prove her point. She opened the robe, revealing the lush, voluptuousness of her body. The body that had gotten her more men than she could count.

The expression in Peter's face revealed that her first attack was making its point. She moved, stepping forward in such a way that it was impossible for the man not to react to what he saw. Paula knew her power over men, she knew the Power her body had over them.

"You can't turn this down, and you know it, Peter," she told him in a throaty voice, stopping only inches from him. "You can't." Her hands cupped under her breasts. "You can't refuse those...to touch, to kiss, to make love to my body. You know how good it is between us. That's the most important thing in the world. The most important thing you'll ever have!"

She threw her arms around him, crushed her body sensually against his. "I love you, Peter. I need you. I won't ever let you go!" And it was the truest thing she had ever said. "I can't let you go!"

Her voice was suddenly desperate. Suddenly frantically anguished. The very idea of what he had suggested was impossible to accept. All at once it hit her, feeling the stiffness of his form against hers, as if he were made of stone.

"Paula...please..."

"Peter...Peter...don't...don't do this!" she cried, tears welling unexpectedly in her eyes. "Don't!''

She was kissing his neck, his cheek, wildly, excitedly, frantically. Then she moved her kisses to his mouth, covering his lips with hers, probing with her tongue. He remained unresponsive for only a brief moment. Then his mouth opened and she thrilled to the power she had over him.

He would never leave her! He couldn't—even if he wanted to.

The kiss lasted a moment and then he shoved her away, violently.

"No—Paula. It won't work! It's finished! We

never were anything more than kicks! You were the kick girl...nothing more! Can't you understand that?" he cried.

"Peter..." She flung her arms around hi neck, once again crushing herself to him. Her hips moved intimately against his. "Make love to me...make love to me...I need you, Peter...you're the best! I need you desperately! I can't...couldn't go on without you! Oh, God, Peter...please...oh, God!" she moaned. But the man remained cold and stiff, waiting for her to finish. Slowly, painfully, Paula slipped away. She stared at him for a moment and then ashamed, sick inside, she turned and rushed into the bedroom, slamming the door behind her. She had never had to plead like that with a man! The shock of having done so, and being blatantly rejected, was too much.

She wasn't even aware of the man leaving the apartment. Emotional tears were streaming down her cheeks.

He can't do this to me! He can't! she screamed over and over again in her mind.

How long she lay there on the bed, sobbing, screaming wild, insane anguish, Paula didn't know. Slowly, as if creeping into a pit of quick sand, she felt herself being dragged down deeper and deeper into an emotional numbness. Finally she sat up in bed, dazed, sick.

Getting up, Paula went into the kitchen, Got herself a stiff shot of whiskcy, and downed it. Pouring another, she fought the bitterness eating itself through her.

What the damn hell right did he have to turn her down? That no good son-of-a-bitch! He was nothing.

Men…men fell at her feet. Men went crazy for her body. No man was going to do this to her! Not Paula Martin!

She gulped the second drink of whiskey. The liquor burned her throat, hit upwards toward her head.

Another stiff drink. Then as she poured the fourth, Paula felt the fury building tightly through her.

Suddenly the glass flew through the air like a rocket. The sound of it hitting the far wall of the kitchen and then bouncing back abruptly broke off as the glass slammed back at Paula. She felt the impact hit the side of her head. For a dazed moment she stood there, numbed, sick. Then shaking herself, Paula reached for the bottle of whiskey and gulped from it. With every swallow she thought about what Peter was attempting to do. She had taken his crap, had taken every agonized word from him. She had listened and comforted him, made love to him, given her body to him, willingly, at call. And now this. He didn't have the right. No man had the right to do that No man would get away with it.

The whiskey was turning into a solid dizzy blur in her body. The world was flaring up into a hateful red haze.

Paula staggered into the living room, fell on the large overstuffed chair, the bottle still clutched in her hand. She gulped from it and the blur of reality slipped further away

What was happening to her that she couldn't hold a man? Or was it because she had never held a man— not the kind that wanted to get married. Maybe she was the kind that men slept with, then dumped.

But she loved Peter Scott. She loved him so

damned much and wasn't about to lose him, no matter
what. She would rather be dead. Would rather see him
dead. Nobody was going to have him—if she couldn't
have him.

The violence of years, the hate, the anguish, the
pain that had driven her from man to man, desperately
searching for something she wasn't even aware of,
something she didn't even know she was looking for,
now knifed through every nerve.

She drank more whiskey and the world continued
to blur, continued to get redder with hate and drunkenness. Everything was spinning and she was in a world
of confusion, of emotion and hate. The love she felt for
Peter Scott now turned into something else that she
didn't understand and didn't try to understand.

And the drinks continued to down the dryness that
kept coming back to her constricted throat. Emotional
tears streamed down her cheeks, pain hammered her
head until she thought she would scream.

When unconsciousness slammed over her, Paula
didn't know. When she awakened again, her hand
automatically raised the bottle to her lips and she
gulped until the desert dryness had ebbed away.

She thought about Peter Scott, about how he dared
to turn her down, to kick her aside, how he had dared
to say he was finished with her—after all they had
meant to each other.

No, to hell with Peter. If she couldn't have him—
nobody would—nobody in the world would have him!

She gulped more whiskey until the red haze
clouded over everything, and left only raw hateful
emotions.

When she got up from the chair, how she got

dressed, where she got the knife, or how she'd managed to get into the car, Paula didn't know. But she was driving, and did know exactly where and why. It all seemed so logical. So simple. Peter would understand, once he saw how serious she really was about him. It would change everything. How could a man turn a woman like her down? No *man* could—and get away with it. No *man* would ever turn her down!

* * * * * * *

Peter had taken Ann out to dinner after work.

They sat in a quiet booth, talking about work, talking about the political situation, talking about important and unimportant things. It wasn't until dinner was finished that Ann asked: "How'd things come out between you and...Paula?"

Peter hesitated, said: "Lousy—but...1 guess she understands, now." He told her about the scene that had taken place in the other woman's apartment.

Ann said: "I'm sorry...I only hope you know what you're doing."

"I know exactly what I'm doing, Ann," he said reaching for her hand. "If you think I'm crazy or not...I'm falling in love with you."

She looked away from him for a moment, then her eyes leveled with his. "Peter...if you really mean that..."

"I mean it."

"I hope you...you do...I couldn't stand being hurt again," she told him in an emotional voice. "Listen to me. I'm getting emotional, now. Let's get out of here."

When they were in the car, Peter turned, looked at

Ann, asked: "Any place in mind?"

"No."

"Drive?"

Ann was thoughtful for a moment, then laughingly said: "Don't you have some etchings you want to show me?"

He blinked, surprised, not quite sure what she was saying at first, and not quite sure she was serious. It was the unexpected that had caught him off base. Then he laughed. Patted her cheek. "Why you know...I do have some etchings at that!"

* * * * * * *

Paula was waiting for them, in her car, outside of Peter Scott's apartment. It had been a long, dry wait, and cigarettes had followed cigarettes. Her nerves were to the point of shattering. Would he never get home? How she needed a drink! Nobody would even turn her down!

Then she saw the car driving up toward her, then it turned into the driveway.

Paula started as she saw Ann Fenneran sitting in the car beside the man, looking happy and extremely intimate.

The fury burst up through Paula, but she held herself there, gripping the car wheel tighter, biting her lower lip until it hurt terribly. There could be a good, dramatic moment to break in on them. Wait until they had gotten settled. Give them time, and then explode on the scene.

Paula's mind was a little blurry, it moved along the line of reasoning, blind to all else. All she could think of was that she needed Peter Scott.

She waited there, her hands shaking, her lips trembling, her visions almost blurred against the anguish spurting up through her.

Finally, how long, she wasn't quite sure, Paula slipped out of the car and headed toward Peter Scott's apartment.

* * * * * * *

The minute the door had closed behind them, Peter found himself pulling Ann into his arms, covering her lips with kisses. It was as if a wildness, an emotional insanity had overcome him, and the woman responded. They locked violently together. But it was more than a passionate embrace. It was an emotional embrace, a release, from waiting, from wanting to hold her close, but not able to until this very moment. And when they finally pulled away from each other, his lips trembled, stumbled over the words that flood from somewhere deep in his heart.

"Oh, I love you...love you...more than...anything... love you so damned much, Ann!" he said, crushing her closer, looking down into her bright blue eyes, thrilling to the sight of her dimpled lips, her short, fluffy blonde hair which made him want to caress and kiss it and her.

Her eyes met his and they seemed to reflect all that he was telling her. Finally her lips moved, softly murmuring, "I love you, too, Peter!"

They embraced again, and were just about to kiss one another when there was a frantic knocking on the door beside them.

Startled, they stiffened, gazed questioningly into one another's eyes.

She mouthed, "Ignore it!" without making even a whispering sound.

But the knocking continued, like the clanging of China Gongs.

Peter sighed, said: "Yes, who is it?"

Only more pounding answered.

He shrugged and then made the mistake of opening the door.

//<u>Chapter Nineteen</u>\\

When Peter Scott looked into the face of Paula Martin, something happened to him, something that he might never have thought possible. It was as if he were looking at his whole life, everything he had done up to that moment, and it all seemed foolishly ridiculous, unimportant. Unimportant, like all the lovers in Paula Martin's life. He looked at the woman and saw, to some extent, his own useless life that spread out behind him like a meandering tired river going no place.

Then shocked surprise settled in when the large woman shoved herself into the apartment.

The door slammed as Paula kicked it shut with her foot. She rammed her fists on her hips, glared at Peter and then Ann Fenneran.

There was a long, too long, stony silence which wrapped around Peter like a clammy hand, choking, stifling his breath, trapping the air in his lungs.

It was several seconds before anybody said anything.

Paula started to open her mouth, and then Peter quickly cut her short.

"What do you want!" he snapped, taking the offensive.

"Well, now, isn't that a sweet little line!" Paula

snapped in a high-pitched voice, her eyes narrowing, her shoulders seeming to lean forward, as if she were getting ready for a spring.

Instantly Peter realized what a mistake he'd made. There was something terribly wrong here.

Ann Fenneran was first to actually recover from the shock. She said: "Why, hello, Paula. I haven't seen you for a long time and—"

"Shut up!" Paula screamed. "You little bitch. What right do you have to step in and try taking my man from me?"

"I'm nobody's man!" Peter snapped, irritated.

"You're a little tramp, that's what you are," Paula stated to Ann, ignoring Peter.

"Hold on!" Peter cried, as the larger woman started to take a step toward Peter.

Without warning Paula moved, so fast, so unexpectedly, with such power for a woman, that he was left stunned. She swung her arm, the hand, holding the purse, hitting the side of Peter's head, like a sledge.

The impact stunned and knocked him backwards, off his balance.

What happened at that point, Peter wasn't quite aware. But the moment he recovered, he found Paula swinging at Ann.

The smaller woman ducked and then twisted away from Paula.

Peter leaped forward, grabbed and then jerked her around by the shoulder.

"What the hell!" he screamed.

One look in Paula's eyes warned him. He immediately cooled his temper, turned to Ann, said: "I better talk to Paula, alone!"

Ann nodded, went into the bedroom, slamming the door behind her.

"Okay, let's just calm down!"

Paula's breath was heavy, her eyes wide, the pupils large.

"You can't do this to me!" she finally hissed out.

"I'm not doing anything to you, Paula."

She laughed. It was a high-pitched sound, edging on the point of a scream.

"What right do you have to kick me aside?" she yelled at him. "I love you! I need you, Peter...you should know that! I'll do anything for you any-thing...for God's sake—get rid of that bitch in there and..."

Peter's mind was thinking fast. He had to get rid of Paula, put her off, someway. He nodded. "I can't just dump her...not right like this...let me set her down easy..."

Paula's face hardened and then she said in a threatening voice: "Get rid of her—and now! I won't have any man of mine knocking around with a bitch like her!"

"That'll do!"

"Nothing will do! You and me and—"

"No...Paula...no..."

The woman's eyes narrowed. "You don't fool me, Peter...not in the least! You're trying to put me off—so you can bang her! That's all you want. Bang women one after another...not caring how they feel, how they care! You're just like all the other men!" All this time she was moving across the room and now slipped into the kitchen.

Peter stood in the middle of the living room, considering how the hell he was going to get out of the situation, not guessing what Paula might be up to.

Then suddenly there was sound in the kitchen of a drawer opening, and he jerked to action.

In one moment he was upon her, his right hand reached out and gripped her left wrist, that held the knife, ready to switch it to her other hand.

For a longtime, which couldn't have been more than a few seconds, they stood staring at one another, then slowly Paula relaxed.

"What's gotten into you, Paula?" Peter demanded, sighing relief, taking the knife from her.

Her eyes narrowed for a moment and then she seemed to grow smaller as her shoulders sagged.

Without a word, Paula started out of the kitchen, her eyes flashed toward the bedroom door behind which Ann had disappeared.

"You haven't heard the last from me," she yelled, loud enough so that Ann could hear.

With that Paula opened the front door and slammed it shut.

* * * * * * *

It took Paula only a few minutes to get to a phone. She dialed and then waited. When the ringing came to a stop and a man's voice said:

"Hello?" she had to hold back a sob of relief.

"Ed," she breathed.

"Yes?"

"I want to warn you...either you fire Ann Fenneran and Peter Scott, or I tell Diana everything I know about you! Everything!" Her voice was high pitched, near the point of hysteria.

"What's wrong?"

"None of your damned business!" she screamed through the receiver. "You fire them, or I'll see to it that your marriage is really finished!" There was a long silence, then Ed said in a stony voice, "I don't know what's wrong with you, Paula, but it won't do any good. I can't just fire somebody without cause. And, anyway, they're too important to the company."

"It's up to you, Ed...one long conversation with Diana and—"

"Nothing would happen. I told Diana everything. We were almost finished, anyway! I thought you knew about that. The worst is over and—"

Paula hung up the phone. Staring blankly at the receiver and then suddenly remembered Tom Kelbore. Tom had the hots for her, but good. As long as she could remember Tom had wanted her. There had been a short affair, because it suited her purposes, some time before. She had broken it off. Tom would jump at the chance and do anything to have her—anything at all.

She put some money into phone box and then dialed again. This time a sleepy butler answered the phone.

"Is Tom there," Paula asked.

"It's late and—"

"If he's there, tell him Paula Martin wants to talk to him!" she snapped.

After a moment of silence the man sighed, said he would see. A few minutes later, Tom was on the other end of the line.

"Yes," he said, carefully.

160

"Tom, I want to see you! Now! It's important!"

After a moment of hesitation he said: "Where?"

"Over there?"

"Can't...there's a party going on—business. But I could slip away," he offered.

"My place, then!"

"Fine, be there in a...thirty minutes!"

* * * * * * *

Paula had rushed to her apartment, fairly ripped off her clothing. She would have to handle Tom just right, feed his ego enough...and then ask the favor. Maybe it was only his body that she had to feed.

She put on a house robe over her naked body and then waited. A drink cooled her nerves and settled the grinding pain in her stomach. It seemed hours, but couldn't have been more than a few minutes before the front door bell rang. She jumped, rushed to the door, flung it open and Tom stepped in, his eyes taking the situation in one quick glance.

He was a mountain of a man, huge broad shoulders, and massive muscles. Dark, brooding features.

His features narrowed as she closed the door behind him. His eyes passed over Paula's body, stopped at the largeness of her breasts.

"Well, Paula," he said; it was a half question, half statement.

"Let's not talk..." she murmured, throwing her arms around his neck.

For a moment the man remained still and unresponsive, and then, slowly, as if made of melting wax, he blended against her, covering her lips with his own.

161

The kiss was deep arid passionate. When they came up for air, he stared down at her, a crooked grin on his lips.

"What's all this about?" he inquired, surprised. "All of a sudden, after so long a time."

She shrugged, twisted around and wiggled across the room. "Maybe I wanted something...but I'm willing to pay...anything you want!"

"What is it?" he asked, his voice harsh.

"Does it matter?" she countered. "We can talk about it later!"

He laughed and then came up to her, his hand pressed her breasts as he pulled her back against him. She felt the clamp of his lips and then the bite of his teeth against the white cream of her throat.

Paula shivered, knowing what was going to happen, hating it, but realizing that this was the price she must pay to get even with Peter Scott. The hands squeezed cruelly at her breasts, and she choked down a moan of pain.

The man suddenly twisted her around and then glared down at her. "You are lovely, Paula. You do things to me...real good things. You got the tits like no other woman I've ever known!" His hand reached out and grabbed hold of her shoulder. His other hand folded around one of her breasts, his lips crushed against her full, large lips, cutting into the soft flesh.

When they broke away again, the man pulled her robe from her body, then grabbing hold of her wrist, jerked her toward the bedroom. "Like you say, we talk later! I've waited a long, long time...wanting you...and now you are going to know it! You're going to like being taken by a real live man who really knows how to treat a woman!" His hand swung out and hit into her fanny. It wasn't a love pat, it was a cruel suggestion as to what would happen in the next minutes in her bedroom.

When Paula heard the bedroom door slam behind the man, as she sank down onto the large double bed, she felt a sickening pain grip the pit of her stomach. She felt like a cheap whore. There had been many times in the past when men had taken her, brutally, in a way, but never like this man, never like Tom Kelbore. Once before they had ended up in bed and for days afterwards her body had ached with the bruised sores of his lovemaking. He took a woman like he was a charging Super Chief, running over the helpless car that had stalled on the tracks, not caring who got hurt. But even then she had not felt like a cheap tramp, a prostitute. This time it was different. Something had happened to her in the last weeks, something she didn't quite understand fully, except in a vague way that involved love for Peter Scott. Her love for him was so complete, that even the idea of bedding down with any other man was repulsive—Tom Kelbore far more terrible than any other she could think of.

But she would bed down with Tom every night, until she got what she wanted, and even that wouldn't be too high a price to pay.

The man moved down to her, his hard body crushing against her own, uncaring, and cruel. His hands would bruise her breasts, his lips would scar her flesh, his body would take hers, hurting, hitting, and inflicting all the terrible pains of brutal love he could manage.

And as he began making love to her, his own special brand of love, Paula felt the anguish rip at her, both physical and emotional. She hated him and hated herself, and hated the world that had made her the way she was. There was nothing wrong in being loved, in having a family, in having children, a husband, and a home. Never before had she really wanted that! Never before had she really, honestly considered marriage as a way of life. Up until now, her life had been one series of love affairs, taking men, using them, having them do what she wanted, when she wanted it. Now she didn't care about anything. She only wanted Peter Scott, and he could never be hers now. She knew that. And revenge was all that was left for her.

The pain slashed at her, time and again, physical, brutal, cutting, hitting pain as the man's thrashing body assaulted hers.

Paula moaned, felt her cut lips trembling, her body rebelling against the demanding, hard form that used her like some kind of unfeeling machine.

There was nothing tender, nothing lovely or wonderful. She felt sensations, but they were only automatic sensations, over which she had no control. But they weren't the kind of pleasure feelings that went through her when possessed by a good lover, rather mere sexual reactions to what was happening to her. All her mind could think about was what she would say afterwards.

And won't he ever be finished?

Finally it ended and she felt the man move away from her and she experienced a deep rush of relief. It was over! Finished! How she hated him! How she hated every man who had used her body. How many had there been in the past? How many of those men had merely been using her, as Peter Scott had used her? How many had fooled her into thinking that she was the one pulling all the strings?

The emotion welled up through her, the hate, the anguish, and the pain. It was far more than physical torture.

Slowly she turned and looked down at the man lying next to her.

How she hated him! Hated him with every inch of her being. He had used her body, not caring what his actions did to her, not caring if she enjoyed herself, not caring if he hurt her!

Rage welled up through Paula in wave after uncontrolled wave.

He was a bastard! But he would do what she wanted. She had a body that all men wanted to possess, even if for only a night! And that was her weapon.

"Tom," she murmured throatily, reaching out and forcing herself to caress his chest with the tips of her fingers.

The man stirred and then his eyes flicked open, looked up at her. His lips curled into a sneering grin. "Now the payoff, Paula?"

There was something in the man's eyes that frightened Paula. But she ignored it.

"Could you do me a favor?" she asked, smiling. "It's such a little favor!"

His eyes mocked her. "What is it?"

"About Peter Scott...couldn't you see that he gets fired?"

He sat up, his grin grew broader, his lips twisted downwards at the corners. "Now how could I do that?"

"Simple enough. Just see to it that his relationship with your father breaks down. That would finish Peter Scott!"

"What would happen then?"

Paula shrugged. She couldn't tell the man that then she would be able to get Peter back—get him in her arms. He would have the job again, if he wanted it— and if he didn't...well, she had enough money for both of them. And money wouldn't matter, anyway, as long as she had Peter!

Tom Kelbore laughed, then. His eyes, his mouth, his whole face laughed at her. "Why would I want to do that?"

"Because I asked you!" she announced in a dangerous voice, feeling the hate and fury threaten its way up through her.

"No dice! Just be a nice girl...lay here and ask me something else...and maybe I'll do something nice for you!"

"What could you do!" she demanded in a whisper. But she knew the answer to that. "Wait a minute...I'll be right back."

It seemed all so logical now that she thought of it. Paula got up from the bed, went into the kitchen, opened a drawer. A few moments later she returned to the bedroom, her eyes calm, distant, her face relaxed, bland. Her hands were behind her as she stepped over to Tom's side of the bed and stood over him.

"I have something for you, Tom," she murmured in a seductive voice.

The man's face brightened and then he laughed. "I bet you do!" His arms reached up to pull her down to him.

She moved like some jungle cat, swift but very calm. Her body lowered, as if to slip down into his arms, then her right hand came around in full sight of the man. The knife she was holding gleamed in the semi-darkness. Then the point plunged into the soft flesh of his stomach. She pulled the handle sideways, so that the sharp blade made a nice neat slice across his belly, drawing a deep line of blood red.

The man screamed only once and then slumped into unconsciousness.

Paula stood, looking at what she had done, then smiled slowly down at him. "How do you like *my* kind of love-making...now?"

But, of course he didn't answer, and never would.

Now, Paula thought, she had a gift for another man. Mr. Scott would probably be just as surprised.

//Chapter Twenty\\

Peter Scott was in that half world between consciousness and unconsciousness. He couldn't be sure if he were actually asleep or awake. But his thoughts were logical and reliving what had happened a few hours before.

They were about Ann and himself, as they had been in each other's arms, making love in a way he hadn't experienced ever before. There was a maturity he had never know with another woman; a maturity of love and emotion. The mere act of sex had little meaning in itself without the emotions being involved. He had realized that at the peak of ecstasy when their bodies had felt the voluptuous sensations of love surge between them. His love was complete and *full,* for Ann had made it something more than physical union, and in a way he had understood the meaning of blending body and soul. They talked about marriage, and were planning on getting married, as soon as possible. The only thing that worried Peter was Ann's insistence they quit their jobs and he go to work for his father. "We want nothing to remind us of Paula Martin and..."

"What are you afraid of?" he countered, angrily.

"Nothing—but...what's wrong with working for your father?"

168

He had tried to explain, but it all seemed foolish and forced, even in his own ears. Finally Ann had said that it might be better if they thought a little more seriously about marriage. Hold off; wait a while. She didn't want a little boy who was trying to prove himself for no purpose.

It hadn't been a fight, exactly, and they had even kissed before going off to sleep. But it had left an awkward wall between them.

He turned his thoughts away from that and tried to settle them on something easier to consider. He thought about the loveliness of Ann, he relived the caresses, the kisses, and the soft wonderful thrill of her pressing up under him. His thoughts relived the hours with Ann Fenneran, thinking about the marriage they had planned. She had tried to talk him into quitting his job and going to work with his father. She had said it would be better to start there, to build a life on what he had, rather than trying to fight the world for no purpose. "You don't have anything to prove with me, Peter," she had told him. Yet, he still wanted something more. Marriage with Ann didn't seem all there was. He couldn't help thinking that there was more in life. Yet he loved Ann more than anything in the world.

Then, suddenly, something jarred him out of the fantasy that had been so real some hours before, and into full consciousness.

His eyes jerked opened. He turned, looked at Ann, who was lying on the bed next to him. Her eyes flickered open and then she sat up.

They both stared at one another for a long time, puzzled.

Then a ringing sounded from the living room.

Peter shifted his gaze to the bedroom door, then to the clock on the bedstand at his left. The luminous dial read 3:30.

"What the hell!" he muttered.

The ringing continued, this time as if somebody had decided to lean on the bell until he came and answered it.

"Hold on your shirt!" he yelled loud enough so that who ever was ringing would stop.

Silence answered him and he sighed his relief. "I'll be right back!" he told Ann, as he opened the bedroom door.

Ann called out: "You're naked!"

"Oh!" Absently he went to his closet and picked out his morning robe, flinging it around his body as he started for the living room.

"Who is it?" he asked as he stepped up to the front door.

Silence answered him and then he sighed, opened the door.

What stood there before him was more startling than if it had been some monster from a horror film.

Paula, her hair hanging loose over her shoulders a house robe tightly wrapped around an obviously naked body. Her right hand was raised above her head, a long, blood covered knife held in her hand. The look in her eyes was bland without expression, as if she were sleepwalking.

Peter didn't have time to react before the woman leaped at him, a loud scream uttering from her mouth.

He couldn't believe what was happening. Happiness within his grasp, perfection. Everything was in order, organized for the first time in his life.

Then the arm fell downwards, the knife reaching out toward his chest.

He tried to tell himself that this wasn't happening, that this was the nightmare, the horror dream.

Then he moved, automatically. But not fast enough.

Paula's large body followed the knife, which reached deep into his side, painfully cutting into the soft flesh under his ribs.

He felt himself falling backwards, then he hit the floor and the woman's body tangled with his.

He heard a whimpering sound coming from Paula's mouth, a sobbing, anguished sound. Then another pain lanced playfully through him as the woman withdrew the knife.

Peter knew that he was facing death, that maybe he was already dying. Yet something quite basic lanced at his mind.

Life, no matter how short was worth fighting for, and his muscles, weakened, moved into action.

He found the woman's wrist, his fingers squeezed, attempted to twist the arm backwards, away from him.

The knife pressed against the center of his stomach and he felt the point prick into his flesh.

God she's strong, he thought. *Insanely strong!*

The world was spinning around him in a reddish haze, falling in and out of focus. He tried to strengthen his grip on Paula's wrist, attempted to lift her bodily from him, to push her weight off the point of the knife.

It seemed an eternity, this struggle for life. The wound in his side was a splitting pain that kept the world of reality distant and dreamlike. His mind kept playing over the events of the last weeks, the childish games of passion he had enjoyed, and was now paying for. It didn't seem possible that Paula Martin could turn out like this, that she would become a woman of hate and violence. He had believed her a fun and games girl who wouldn't care if the man called it off. Now he realized that no matter what kind of attitude she had projected, the truth was that Paula, above all other women, was the type who could not stand to be turned down. She had played the tough game with men—but couldn't stand that kind of game played on her. And he'd been honest, fair, and decent about it with her. How could he have guessed?

Suddenly he saw himself for what he was, for what he had been trying to do. Prove himself to himself! Ego. Nothing seemed so important. Now he realized that it wasn't important at all. The only thing that mattered was his life with Ann. His future with Ann. He wanted to marry her, to have a family with her, buy a nice little house. Who could want more? What else was there beyond family and home? Fame and money were shallow against such happiness. Peter realized that nothing was important other than Ann and himself and the way they lived together for the rest of their lives.

But he didn't have much time, and maybe no time at all. Maybe his life was being torn away from him right now. Maybe he wouldn't live more than a few minutes!

Sickness ripped up at him.

He didn't want to die. He only wanted Ann. Facing death, now, he realized that life and living was the only thing important. What had happened in the past wasn't that important. He could only have the future.

172

Nobody should live in the past, nobody should go around trying to prove themselves to anybody. If they are happy, if they have somebody to love them, there is nothing else that is important.

Give me life! his mind screamed.

Oh, God, there were so many things he wanted to tell Ann. So many things that mattered, that were important to him. Love. Oh, how beautiful it could be. No matter what! And he might have lost everything again, if he'd let his driving passion to get ahead blind him to what was truly important.

He struggled against the probing knife that threatened to take everything away from him.

How long he continued pressing up against Paula, he didn't know. It seemed forever to his pain-filled mind. The burning at his side was growing hotter and hotter, his strength seemed to be ebbing away faster and faster.

Suddenly he felt the knife dig deeper and then with all his strength, Peter pushed upwards, knowing that this would be his final effort to escape death.

The woman's form lifted, the knife pressure slipped away. Peter jerked, twisting with all his strength. He wanted to live more than anything in the world, he wanted to live with Ann, have children. Nothing was more important than that.

He fought for survival and didn't think that about this being a woman who was in a life and death battle with him.

The body lifted away from him, it flung against the floor and he twisted with all his strength on the arm that was still held in his hands.

Then he saw Ann Fenneran standing over them,

high-heeled shoe in her hands. She swung down on Paula's head and the other woman slumped.

It was several moments before anybody moved.

Then Ann came down into his arms. She cried:

"Oh, Peter...I'll do anything you say. Anything. We'll continue to work at the firm...we'll do anything you want...just so I have you...and that's all that matters!"

Peter smiled to himself as he touched Ann's forehead with his lips. "No, you were right, Ann. It's better to start from the beginning...and away from everything that brought us together. The company can do without us. I'll call Dad up tomorrow and...I'll make...arrangements to...to..."

His voice faded out and he felt the world fading. But in a way it seemed merely as if the past were fading, as if what he had once been was fading. The future would be his for the taking, with Ann as his wife.

The blackness was only a few moments, so it seemed to Peter Scott, but when he opened his eyes, he was lying in bed, Ann was sitting next to him, his parents were at the foot of the bed.

Ann smiled. "You don't have to say a thing, Peter. I arranged everything." Then she told him that the police had discovered Tom Kelbore dead in Paula Martin's apartment when they'd gone there with her to get a few things before taking her to the station for booking.

"The poor girl!" Peter sighed.

"They say something's mentally wrong with her..." Ann told him. "At least, that seems to be their attitude towards her. Maybe...maybe things will work out. I talked to Ed, and he didn't like the idea of you quitting, but said he understood, under the circumstances. And anyway, Kelbore has all the information he needs for his new line. You at least proved you could!"

Peter smiled. "It all seems unimportant, now. I have you!" Then, as he reached out and grabbed her hand, he looked at his parents, "And you, too, now. I think we'll have that Scott and Son on the store again, Dad."

"And, maybe, grandson," Ann pointed out, laughing.

//<u>About the Author</u>\\

Charles Nuetzel was born in San Francisco in 1934, and writes:

"As long as I can remember I wanted to be a writer. It was a dream I never thought would materialize. But with the help of Forrest J Ackerman, who became my agent, I managed to finally make it into print.

"I was lucky enough not only in selling my work to publishers but also ending up packaging books for some of them, and finally becoming a 'publisher' much like those who had bought my first novels. From there it as a simple leap to editing not only a science-fiction anthology, but also a line of SF books for Powell Sci-Fi back in the 1960s. Throughout these active professional years I had the chance to design some covers and do graphic cover layouts for pocket books & magazines."

Much of his work in covers and graphics are a result of having had a father who was a professional commercial artist, and who did a number of covers for sci-fi magazines in the 1950s and later for pocket books—even for some of Mr. Nuetzel's books.

In retirement he has become involved in swing dancing, a long time lover of Big Band jazz. But more interestingly world travels have taken him (and his wife Brigitte) across the world, to Hawaii, Caribbean, Mexico, Kenya, Egypt, Peru, having a lifelong interest in ancient civilizations. His website is full of thousands of pictures taken during these trips.